The tale of Naomi, the Greatest Hero of Mai

By Herman Harrison

THE TALE OF NAOMI THE GREATEST HERO OF MAI

© 2024, Herman Harrison

Edited by Herman Harrison

Cover art by Herman Harrison

To give questions, comments, or concerns regarding this book,

please contact: mannyh12982@gmail.com

Ebook ISBN:9798227339379

Paperback ISBN:9798227620101

HERMAN 1 HARRISON

I

Heroes of Mai

"Before thoughts were thought of, there was

nothing. And before that, there was Oritula Tali and Solituno

Tali. These two beings were in existence before anything ever

existed, and were polar opposites from one another. Oritula

Tali, the golden cat, was a spirit of joy, love, determination

and hope, while Solituno Tali, the dark cat, was a spirit of

vengeance, hatred, jealousy and misery. These two spirits

roamed the vast void of nothingness until some point in time,

when they clashed into one another.

"However, this contact was not a peaceful greeting.

The two beings were incomprehensibly powerful spirits, so

much that they could affect the physical world, and when

they made contact, the two created something new. The

two's spiritual energies coming into contact with one another

lead to an unfathomably large and spectacular arrangement

of new creations being brought into existence into the

physical world. First there was water. Then another clash, and

there was earth. Then another, making wind and fire! The

elements were eventually so abundant that when they themselves began clashing into one another, they formed new elements.

"Eventually, over thousands of millennia, Oritula Tali and Solituno Tali's spirits were so energized from all of the elements being formed from them continuously clashing for eons and eons, that they eventually exploded into a gargantuan combustion of light, scattering their spirits all over the universe. Over time these elements began harnessing traits from the cat spirits, and in time there came to be a vast land of varying geography within an endless storming sea of countless sea creatures.

"Over time many intelligent creatures arose from the elements, but the one to conquer all others was the furious Tabby clan, known as the ones that came from nowhere. This is because no Tabby clan member had any elemental properties. This was quite strange, as every other creature had some sort of elemental power deriving from their elements, such as the Fox clan, a clan of canine fire controlling creatures, or the Hawk clan, shapers of lighting. Despite this, the Tabby became the dominant demographic of the large land that formed from the elements.

"In time, the shards of the spirit of Solituno Tali grew stronger and stronger, as more and more evil deeds were being committed in the land formed from the elements. This grew so much in fact, that Solituno was able to just about form into the physical world, in the form of a deep dark purple cougar, with sharp black teeth that could slice the toughest of skin. This "cougar" went around terrorizing the people of the land formed from the elements, destroying villages and ripping families apart, leaving a trail of pitch black suffocating fog behind it.

"However, in one small island village, off the coast of the land, there was a young cat, whose name was Mai. He was Tabby, so no one thought he was worth paying attention to. Still, even when no one saw him, he was always optimistic, and always saw the bright side of things. Now, when Solituno approached Mai's village, the spiritual energy of Solituno had completely covered all of the land, pushing Oritula's spirit fragments to Mai's village.

"Just as Solituno began taking out the last spark of light within the cold, dark land, Oritula's spirit began to revive, as all of its spirit energy fragments had compacted into the small town, close enough to reconnect. This caused a long, extremely bright beam of golden light to shoot from the ground. Now, unlike Solituno, in order for Oritula to survive, she would have to find a body to host, so she could fight the cougar that was really Solituno. This is because the contempt that Solituno embodied was more so connected to the state of the world than the pureness of Oritula, which had long since faded. In that same moment, the golden light bent back down from the clouds and shot straight into Mai. Mai now had the wisdom and power of the embodiment of determination, hope, and joy, Oritula Tali!

"With this power, Mai suddenly felt a strong urge to do what made him the most joyous in that moment - play the drums. Now, unbeknownst to Mai at the time, when one emits the traits of a spirit, it will strengthen them and repel

any spirits of the opposite nature. At that moment, Mai was

nervous, but excited, setting his drum kit outside, and just as

the cougar started approaching him to bite a chunk out of

him, Mai started playing.

"He enjoyed it, he had fun, and the positivity he was

emitting was so powerful that sound booms began to emit

from the drums so powerful that the entire planet began to

vibrate. Eventually the drum kit began to float, and Mai too!

Though he still played, and began to go through a sky dance,

while playing the drums.

"The cougar became extremely weak and fatigued

due to all of the soundwaves of enjoyment and positivity

overwhelming its negative energy. Mai knew that this would

likely be his only chance to defeat the cougar, so he grabbed a

spear and impaled it, instantly breaking it into fragments.

Right as Mai killed the cougar, its body dissipated and spread

out everywhere across the land. The fog disappeared, the

people that died came back to life, and Oritula left Mai's body, spreading herself all across the land, like Solituno.

"When it was all said and done, Mai was thanked for saving everyone, and was celebrated with a mighty festival every year from that day on that lasted 5 days, the same amount of days the cougar terrorized the land! Before he died, Mai prophesied that Solituno would come back, over a long period of time, in a much stronger form, much more difficult to defeat. When Mai died, in honor of him, and to keep his name alive, the land was officially named Mai. That land is the land in which you reside. The land of the hero of Mai!"

Naomi was asleep, laying on the ground, as she usually loved to do, especially during Wisely's long lectures on the history of Mai. She felt like she already knew everything to be known. Wisely looked down from his high view and looked down to see a little orange and white Tabby cat, sleeping on one of his roots. A Tabby cat that fell asleep during his very important lecture.

Wisely spoke, "Naomi, wake up at this instant!"

Naomi was woken up, "*Yawn* Huh...? OH! I'm sorry Wisely, I forgot you were telling me something. You said it was important, or something? What was it?"

"Did you not hear a single thing I just told you?" Wisely's voice creaked.

"Um... no?"

"*Sigh* Well Naomi, the sun is setting. I suppose you might want to start heading home."

"Well, it's only just started to set. I think I'd rather go... to the Seaside Park instead! You know, to see the seagulls... well, do what seagulls do?"

"Naomi. I do find it important that you listen to what I tell you. Advice that I give you may be convenient to have one day."

Naomi was already running on her way to the park, and hadn't heard anything that Wisely had said, "Yeah sure. Well, have a good evening Wisely!"

Naomi arrived at the park within minutes, though it was miles away from where Wisely was. She was excited to go and watch seagulls go… do whatever they do? The park was along a long beach coastline with a supermarket sized surf and turf restaurant named Huardi's with a couple of bright orange chairs stationed out front. Not much, but for Naomi, this was her favorite place to go.

After skipping along the beach, she got to Huardi's, but no one was there. *"Guess Huardi's is closed today."* She began to grin, *"Time to do what I came here to do..."* Naomi entered across a venue, in the back of Huardi's. Within the empty venue there layed no soul nor item, but a single drum kit and drum sticks. Naomi's face lit up as if she had been told she could sleep all day.

She scurried onto the large stage within the black, dimly lit venue and sat on the drum kit seat. Then she started playing. She played for hours and hours, until she finally looked at the time, *"11 PM?! I should head home."* As she left Huardi's she noticed the dark seashore and looked up into the sky. *"Someday I'll be able to play to all sorts of people."* Naomi waddled her way back home and fell face first onto her bed.

The next morning, the glistening light of the sun woke Naomi up in her bedroom, cluttered with TAB sheet music and album posters of her favorite artists piled onto her wall. She was organized, she just never liked throwing things away. Naomi got out of bed, and went out of her house to open her mailbox, which she hadn't done in a while. She opened the hatch and saw a stack of mail so packed it seemed like it would have exploded if it wasn't opened. She went back to her bedroom, layed comfortably in her bed, turned her TV on and started going through her mail. *"Bills... advertisements... ooh, a* check!"

Eventually Naomi came to her last slip of paper. A red velvet envelope with a blue ribbon seal. *"Wonder what this is..."* Naomi opened the envelope and read the paper.

HELLO!

CONGRATULATIONS, NAOMI! YOU HAVE BEEN PICKED TO PERFORM WITH THE WIDELY RENOWNED MUSIC ARTIST, JUNGLE FROG MANNY MOVANIO IN TAMIBA CITY! PACK YOUR DRUMSTICKS, BECAUSE THIS ENVELOPE IS A FREE OLIVIA SKIES PLANE TICKET TO TAMIBA CITY, SET TO LEAVE JANUARY 12TH.

It was January 10th. Naomi only had two days to make the trip.

"Finally! This is my chance! I'm gonna make it big in Tamiba city!"

Naomi had gone to an audition a week ago that would decide who would be the new drummer for Manny Movanio, the creator of a few of Naomi's favorite songs. He needed someone to play for him live, and it seemed Naomi was fit for the job.

Tamiba city was the biggest city in Mai. It was the epicenter of entertainment, and all kinds of species resided within the city's blocks. Naomi scurried through her small home and packed bags. Clothing, snacks, a picture of Wisely, drumsticks. That's all she packed, hoping to stay in Tamiba city. She ate some cold pizza from a couple of days ago and rushed out of the door.

As she opened the door she felt the blistering early morning wind smack her face. She didn't mind though, she liked the cold. Before she left, she had to say goodbye to her closest of pals, Wisely.

"Why, hello Naomi. What brings you here today? Would you like me to tell you the history of our land once more?"

"Um, actually no. I just got some mail that said I was invited to Tamiba City to perform!"

"I'm happy for you, Naomi. I knew you would win the audition!"

"Thanks Wisely! ...Well, I guess I gotta go. I have to catch a flight pretty soon! I'm gonna miss you If I make it big."

"Naomi, I know in time we will meet once more, our destinies are intertwined. So, goodbye for now, and I wish you well in Tamiba City."

"Hmm... well I don't know what you're saying about destiny and stuff, but thanks for the wishes!" Naomi hugged the large tree and began running to the airport.

Naomi arrived at the airport and boarded the plane she was set to fly on. A few minutes later, the plane took flight. In time, the plane arrived at Tamiba City. The plane intercom started screeching.

"HELLO, I HOPE ALL ARE DOING WELL. WE HAVE NOW LANDED IN TAMIBA CITY. PLEASE REMEMBER TO TAKE YOUR BAGS AND EXIT IN AN ORDERLY MANNER."

Naomi scurried through the busy airport filled with all kinds of different creatures.

"Is that a talking bird?? How is FIRE coming out of that fox's mouth??? What kind of place is this?"

Naomi was intimidated by all of the commotion and fast paced procedures she had to go through in the airport. She felt she was in a large snare drum, and it was constantly being hit. Eventually, over the course of about half an hour or so, Naomi finally escaped the airport. As she left the airport, she witnessed the grand spectacle that was Tamiba City. It was well into the night. Bright city lights hung on ginormous buildings, blinking advertisements for all sorts of products. Naomi looked at the envelope once more to find where she was supposed to be.

AT YOUR ARRIVAL, YOU MUST COME TO THE CARITOBA HOTEL. WE WILL BE WAITING!

Naomi, starting to get a little confused by the

HERMAN 15 HARRISON

directions as she had never heard of these places, looked around for a friendly face to ask for help. Out of everyone at the airport plaza she was in, she spotted an albino, bipedal alligator dressed in a shiny dark green blazer with a brown fedora, long brown leather pants and a pair of brown dress shoes. He was reading a newspaper, inattentive to the world around him. Naomi walked up to the gator and introduced herself, "Excuse me?" The gator lifted his head from his newspaper.

"Huh? Oh, hey. What's up?"

"Hello, my name is Naomi. I've come from far away, and I was invited here to perform some songs. I'm not sure if you've heard of them..."

"Naomi? So you're the drummer, right? "

"...How'd you know?!"

"I'm the bassist. Of course I know. Oh! By the way, my name's Makim."

Naomi, surprised at this coincidence, froze for a moment before responding.

"So, Makim, would you happen to know where the Caritoba

Hotel is? I have a letter that says I need to go there. I've never been here before though, so I'm kind of lost..."

"Don't worry, just walk straight down Ritherfend street. That's the street we're on right now. Then, eventually you'll find it. You can't miss it, the sign's in big orange and yellow letters."

Naomi thanked Makim for the help and ventured to the hotel. Along the way she began to feel an off aura coming from the area she was in. Now cautious, she looked around her, and saw all of the locals looking at her in dismay. Petty crimes were being committed right in front of her eyes; people were selling illicit materials, they were stealing, and they were breaking and entering.

Some looked like they were plotting - plotting against Naomi. Naomi grew fearful of what might happen if she stayed outside much longer, and began skipping, still trying to stay cheerful about her opportunity to perform in front of an entire city. Though no one knew it, the spirit of Solituno had been steadily growing stronger within Tamiba City, as malicious intent grew more and more, and crimes rose. This was unbeknownst to Naomi though, as she had never truly listened to Wisely's stories.

Naomi soon arrived at the Caritoba Hotel, and at arrival, was greeted by five eagles in black jumpsuits with small green pins on their chest.

"Your suit room will be on floor 24, hallway B, room 1. Congratulations on being chosen."

They were monotone, no emotions being emitted. This was unnerving to Naomi, who thanked them and went on to her room. *"I'm really happy to be in Tamiba City, I really wanna get some sort of success here, but... why do so many people seem so... off?"* Naomi decided to put her worries to rest and go to sleep. The next day was the day of her performance, after all.

The next day, Naomi jumped out of bed and woke up to the ominous sight of a dark gray sky. Apparently the next few days were going to be cloudy, but Naomi had never seen

such a dark sky in the morning. Naomi made herself breakfast,

practiced the drums on an electric drum set that Manny had

provided in the hotel, and dressed herself in her favorite outfit

- a blue and orange tye-dye kimono. Not exactly ideal for

drumming, but nonetheless, Naomi grabbed her drum sticks,

and left the hotel. Makim was standing outside the hotel, along

with Manny, and they were discussing the plan for what songs

they would be performing.

"Songs…wheather…blah blah…"

Naomi approached them and let them know she was

ready. She greeted Manny, "Hey, it's so nice to meet you! You

know, I knew you were a blue frog, but your color's even

more vibrant in person."

"Thanks, I appreciate it! Well, there's no time to waste

guys, let's go!"

They all set for the stage, which was nearby the

hotel. Naomi got on the stage, in full confidence, and just as

the band was ready to play, the amps they had plugged into

Manny's guitar and Makim's bass busted. The thousands of people waiting for the performance started chattering, wondering what was going on. And on top of that, it started to rain, seemingly out of the blue. The crowd booed and were furious. With such a bad scenario, the timing seemed almost preplanned.

The time was now. Solituno finally had enough negative energy concentrated into one space to take physical form once more. And so they did. It was quite the spectacle in fact. People's boos were halted, as a blindingly bright purple and red light speared through the sky, and a large vein opened in the sky, and out of the vein, came a monstrously ginormous dragon, with a slick body, sharp fangs and pointed scales. Its eyes were as deep red as blood. Such a dreadful, truly horrifying sight. Its pure magnitude brought some citizens to pass out. The dragon's aura left a deep purple haze in the sky, further darkening the sky.

The citizens of Tamiba City were horrified, and began running frantically, in an attempt to run away from the giant beast that was Solituno. But fortunately for them, as this purple haze fell upon them, unlike last time, they did not die. Instead, Solituno gained full control over them. Solituno then infected Manny and Makim. The city blocks were silent. Everyone was frozen still. Except for Naomi. She was the one glimmering light of hope for Tamiba City. Maybe she wasn't infected because she wasn't afraid. Or maybe she was just so excited to play the drums. But no matter what it was, it came in the form of intense positivity, and repelled the effects of Solituno's haze.

"And who is this, this little pest, that refuses to succumb to my control?"

Solituno was able to telepathically communicate with Naomi. Naomi, now fearful, yet boastful, stood brave, and responded to the beast.

"I am Naomi. I come from a faraway land that you probably have never heard of...What is it that you want? What have you done to everyone? What's the meaning of this?!"

Naomi was still staying relatively positive despite the crazy scenario she was in.

"Your aura... It's too powerful for me to control... I see you have drumsticks. Why don't you play for the crowd before you, NAOMI?"

Naomi, initially hesitant and in a slight sweat, was shocked when out of nowhere, Manny and Makim started playing their instruments. But something was off. Something about their eyes were off. It was something about how they played, that was off. There was no humanity in it. No feel. It felt like she was listening to two robots playing instruments. Nonetheless, Naomi saw no choice but to perform for the giant beast, in hopes of not angering it. Naomi played. She played in front of the crowd. They began to boo more than they did before. They ridiculed her and mocked her. When she made mistakes, they would all laugh at her. The taunting was starting to get to her.

This was all part of Solituno's plan, to get into Naomi's head, and to lower her self esteem, make her vulnerable and control her. But Naomi was no soft cookie, and she began to immediately reject those negative thoughts trying to enter her mind, and kept playing.

In fact, she was so bold, she started to genuinely

enjoy playing. She eventually started making extra improvisations on her drum line as she saw fit. She was so happy at that moment, not caring what anyone else said, that she couldn't hear anything else but the drumkit. Then, she was broken out of that zone.

"I see you won't be breaking anytime soon. Well, I have tried to spare your life, but if you are so bold as to go against my control, then I, the embodiment of negativity, Solituno, will consume you, so that you may be of some use to me, by satisfying my long hunger. I haven't eaten in the physical realm for centuries, after all. Mwahaha!!"

Solituno then swooped down to where Naomi was and began gliding towards her at breakneck speeds. And just as Solituno was about to open his mouth to eat Naomi, a gargantuan, blinding light began to shoot out of Naomi's eyes, colored baby blue and white, and she began to float, along with her drums and drumsticks. Then, for Naomi, everything went black.

When Naomi opened her eyes, she saw nothing but

a white void. Naomi understandably began freaking out, but then a voice spoke that, for some reason, instantly soothed her.

"Naomi, do not be afraid. It is I, the embodiment of joy, happiness, peace, positivity."

"What? Wh-what just happened? A giant purple dragon popped out of the sky, I started playing the drums and I started floating and now I'm... here?"

"You are now within a gap between pockets of time. The outside of the physical realm, you could call it. But now is not the time to discuss where you are right now. It is time to discuss where you are going to go."

"Huh? What are you talking about? Who are you?" Naomi scoffed.

"Have I not just told you? I am the embodiment of Positivity. I, am Oritula Tali, The Golden Cat Spirit. I do ask you again, where are you going to go? You must have some idea of where you're going. In life."

Naomi tried to remain calm about the situation she

was in, and answered the best she could, "Future, huh? Well, first off, I'm Naomi, and, uhhh... I plan on being here, in Tamiba City, performing for all of the people of the city, and the world!"

"Heh...such a bright, vibrant soul. I'm glad that I've been able to meet you, Naomi. But now, we have Solituno to deal with."

"Uh huh... And... How do we get rid of that giant dragon? Or, Solituno?"

"There is negative and positive energy. When there's enough of one, the other is repelled, and when it's strong enough, it can be manifested into the physical realm, that being your realm. To put this as simple as I can for you Naomi, In order to defeat Solituno, you and I will have to mend into one another. Become one, so that you may harness all of my energy in the physical realm and rise to greater power than you've ever felt before. When you do this, you'll have powers not even Solituno possesses."

Before Oritula had finished speaking Naomi had

already made up her mind. "Whatever it takes to defeat that monster that's trying to ruin what's supposed to be the best day in my life, I'll do it. I won't let him ruin this day!"

"I WAS HOPING YOU'D SAY THAT. NOW, YOU WILL FALL ASLEEP ONCE MORE, AND WHEN YOU DO, I WILL BE WITH YOU, AND YOU WILL FEEL IT."

"Will do. Oh! I think I heard Wisely talking about you before! Wow, maybe I should listen to him more often...zzzz"

Naomi woke up to the horrifying sight of the giant dragon's mouth beginning to close in on her. At that very moment, Naomi's eyes began to light up, shooting white from one eye, blue from the other, but this time, she did not pass out.

With an electrifying surge of energy rushing all throughout her body, she used the power to punch one of the dragon's teeth out. The dragon backed off, and Naomi began to levitate into the air, and her drums began to float as well, along with her drumsticks.

"Whoa... what's happening Oritula?!?!"

"I AM WITHIN YOU, AND YOU ARE HARNESSING MY POWERS. YOU ARE ABLE TO PLAY THE DRUMS, YES? THEN PLAY THEM. PLAY WHATEVER YOU'D LIKE, AS LONG AS YOU'RE ENJOYING IT. REMEMBER, IT'S THE ENJOYMENT OF WHAT YOU DO THAT WILL DEFEAT SOLITUNO. I BELIEVE IN YOU NAOMI, AND I KNOW YOU BELIEVE IN YOU. THIS IS YOUR DESTINY, TO DEFEAT THE EMBODIMENT OF CORRUPTION ONCE AND FOR ALL!"

"You know what, Oritula? I think you're right. I'm definitely cut out for this job!"

This was the second battle, the battle that would decide who would be the new superior of the realm of Mai. Naomi began playing her favorite song on the drums. Even without a bassist or guitarist playing along she still was able to enjoy her own line of music. She started playing it faster, and faster, and even faster, until she was going at such a speed that she appeared to be nothing but a blur.

"Hah. You think you can do what Mai did to me all those centuries ago? Kid, I won't let that happen again."

Solituno then flew up to where Naomi was, opened his mouth, and consumed her whole.

Little to Solituno's knowledge, however, Naomi was still alive, and she did not stop playing. She kept playing faster and faster. Though she was consumed by the darkness, she kept burning brighter and brighter until she created a vortex of bright light and intense soundwaves that erupted from the drums, shooting everywhere inside of the beast's intestines, ripping it from the inside out."

"Blu—Blur— wh—what is happening to me? What have I done to myself by swallowing that mere tabby? Blurr—wraaghhh!!"

Slivers of light began to pierce through the dragon's thick body and, in a matter of seconds, Solituno's body was torn to grainual pieces, and they all spread all throughout the land of Mai, once more.

The battle was over. The sky cleared and turned deep blue, people snapped back into their normal selves, and there was no more purple haze. Naomi had won the battle.

"Naomi, I do thank you for helping me to defeat Solituno! Without your help, the world would be utterly destroyed. I am in debt to you, as well as all of those that you saved from Solituno's wrath."

"Wow, thank you!"

"I will now dissipate from the surface of your mind for now, and go back into the void, along with Solituno."

"But what if he comes back? People need you to stay! You saw how cool the stuff was that I was doing, right?"

"Haha! Naomi, don't you see...? Unlike last time I battled Solituno, this is different. We are now connected! Besides, it was your positivity that had prevented you from becoming overtaken by the impudence of Solituno. I know you will find my help useful another time, so I will be with you all the rest of your days. Maybe even in the next battle we'll meet once more!"

"Next battle?? Hey, Oritula, what are you talking about?!?"

By now, Naomi noticed Makim snapping his fingers

in front of her face, "Sweetheart, break out of it! Our amps are fixed, we don't need you malfunctioning now!"

"Huh? Oh! Ok, I'm ready to play!"

The crowd, seemingly, had been unfazed by what just happened to them. The crowd cheered and was eager to hear the new band play for the first time.

Manny began the countdown…

"Ok guys, 1…2…3…"

II

Naomi, the Warrior of Mai

You remember what happened to Tamiba city, right?

A little tabby named Naomi came there to have a blast playing the drums for a performance, then next thing you know, a big ole' scary dragon (who's name is Solituno) forms from all of the hatred within the people of Tamiba city! I bet you're scared, right…? Well no need to fear, Naomi was there!

Naomi, being an absolute embodiment of hope and determination, smited Solitunio with the power of her drum playing skills! With each strike of the drum, Solituno was cracked and cracked until they ultimately shattered into a quintillion fold pieces, soaring through the gust in the sky! What happened after that, you say…? Well, I guess we can begin our story here.

THE AFTER THE SOLITUNO BATTLE

Naomi had just woken up from her sleep after a long day of craziness.

"*YAWN* Man, that was a good nap…" She analyzed her

surroundings, waiting for her body to wake up too. *"Dark olive room with a beautiful sky view...the sun's setting already...big TV...*sniff*...tuna croquettes!"* Naomi suddenly mustered the strength to get out of the bed. She tumbled out of her blanket, which was trying its best to keep her trapped in its drowsy inducing grip. She escaped its wrath and managed to make it to the kitchen.

As she expected, a big pile of tuna croquettes were laid out on an especially big plate. But who had made these croquettes? Who made these delicious delicacies our drumming hero is so eager to enjoy? Naomi locked onto a familiar face. It was Makim, the scaley reptilian bassist of Manny's band. "Makim, was this all you?? I didn't know you could cook!"

"Hehe... I see you've finally woken up! I made these for supper, eat all you want, just save some for me."

"Thanks Makim! Time to eat!

"Wait! Before you started eating, I wanted to ask you something."

"Yeah?"

"Well, I was wondering if you knew what you planned on doing, now that you've accomplished your big dream, performing in Tamiba City for Manny? I'm sure you've had some idea of what you want to do, right? A bigger picture in your head...?"

Naomi contemplated, but to her dismay she had not in the slightest ever thought of what she was planning to do next. She didn't even think of the possibility of there being a "next."

"Hm...I'm not sure... I guess I'd keep performing with you and Manny and travel all over Mai? That's it, really. WOW... I really have no long term plan in life. ...Should I be concerned?"

"No, of course not! You're only 19! You know what, I shouldn't have asked that. You've got plenty of time to think of that."

"Yeah, I guess I'll just go wherever the wind takes me."

Naomi and Makim left the hotel and walked the

streets of Mai. As much as they could, that is, before the paparazzi came rushing to Naomi to take her picture and ask her all sorts of questions.

"When did you first know you wanted to play the drums?"

"Where do you buy your clothes from?"

"What do you plan on doing now that you've saved all of Mai from Solituno?"

Naomi and Makim rushed out of the big crowd of impatient interviewers. It didn't take long for them to find a decent hiding spot. They ran into an old dimly lit juke joint. Naomi and Makim panted from exhaustion, but they could feel eyes all over them. They sat at an olive green booth in the corner of the cadet blue juke joint, and-what do you know! Manny just so happened to be there as well! Manny looked up at the two and began to grin.

"Oh, hey guys! I've been looking for you for a while. I know you guys are wondering, 'what happens next?' Well I've been thinking we could go on tour in Calidum City!"

Makim sighed dreadfully, "Calidum City? That old desert village people still call a city? Barely anyone lives there I've heard. Maybe somewhere else... Like Glandes Port City? I've heard they have a whole bunch of big music artists there, and I'm sure going there would give us a bit of a boost of popularity in the Seascape region of Mai."

"No way Makim! I've heard Glandes Port City is packed to the brim with garlicky food! You know how much I don't like garlic. Besides, I've been hearing around from people on the street that there's a lot of stuff I can find out about Solituno in that so-called desert village."

Manny and Makim turned their heads in confusion. Manny queried her statement, "Uh Naomi... didn't you defeat Solituno? I mean I'm pretty sure that the dragon's not coming back, especially after you shattered it into oblivion."

Naomi's demeanor turned extremely serious, "Manny... If Solituno came back after all this time, don't you think they'll come back again in the far future? I need to make sure that if that happens again, I tell people what they need to know to stop them. You might be right... but might as well, right? My friend Wisely from back home always told me I should read more anyways!"

Manny nodded in agreement, "I understand. Anyways, it seems like it's two to one Makim! So pack your bags, I already booked a flight at Olivia Skies, so we're leaving tomorrow!" Makim slumped back to the hotel with Naomi and they both packed their bags. One moving at swift speeds, fantasizing of future adventures. Another moving slow as a snail, pouting to themselves non-stop, "It's going to be so hot... I don't look good sweating...I can't stand the desert..."

The next day, the gang rushed to the airport and got on their flight. They all sat together, and of course, Naomi got the window view. Manny ate a large breakfast of fruit, so he spared his gut of the flavorless snacks the flight provided.

Makim however, had not eaten, and with his stomach begging for fuel to carry on his life, he got the attention of a lovely dove flight attendant, who was smiling at everyone she crossed her eyes with, "Excuse me ma'am?" The dove initially saw Manny and smiled.

That being said, to Makim and the gang's surprise, when she realized it was Makim that had called her over, her face turned from the most lovely of faces to see in the sky, to the most wretched of faces, a face of hatefulness, a face of evil. The intimidating face alone must not have been enough for Makim to stop right there and realize there was a problem, "Hello, can I please have some olive flavored gummies? I've heard they have quite a unique taste-" Makim was very rudely interrupted by the dove.

"We don't serve those here. we literally haven't sold those since LAST YEAR! GOSH... your crocodilian people find a way to threaten the entirety of Mai, yet you can't even keep up to date on the simplest of things!" Clearly, this dove was not a dove of peace. At least not with Makim or anyone who was associated with Makim, for that matter.

"Hey, keep it down a notch, won't ya? You don't have to be so nasty just because you don't like your job. Aren't you supposed to be a symbol of peace?"

"…Don't you know what his own have done to Mai? I mean, you saved Mai. You must know, of all people, how wretched his people are." The dove turned back to Makim, "You can pretend all you want. You can play this 'acting game' you're playing for all your friends as long and as well as you'd like. But know very well, there are so many people who aren't fooled by your act. I know who you are. I know where you come from. From the embodiment of destruction."

"Alright bud, chill out, ok? We don't want olive gummies anymore, just leave us alone…" The dove scoffed and went on her way.

"Makim, what was she so mad about?"

"I have no idea! I've never met that dove in my life! And I'm not even a croc! I'm a gator!"

"Hm… Well maybe being this high up in the sky for so

long has gotten to her head."

The gang chuckled, and dismissed the oddly aggressive encounter. And of course, Naomi was the first one to fall asleep. Makim and Manny fell asleep soon after. That night, Makim dreamed about olives.

The plane landed along with the setting of the moon and the rise of the sun, and along with the sun rose the gang. When entering the airport, they were met with the sweet smell of lavender. When they left the airport, they could not believe their eyes. It was a literal desert village.

The small huts the village consisted of were entirely made of sand, and if that weren't strange enough, even the clothing of the townspeople were sand garments. How they stayed intact was a mystery.

Manny knew the town might not be the biggest, but he didn't expect the town to be small enough to see its entirety from one angle. Besides, why would an airport be right next to such a seemingly remote part of Mai?

Despite this initial confusion, the group stayed

confident, and began exploring the area in hopes of finding someone who knew any good spots to perform at. Unfortunately there were only a small number of reptilian townspeople.

Manny tagged along with Makim, who made conversation with an old crocodile elemental, "Hello sir, my name is Makim, and I came with two others because we'd 'love' to perform for you in this lovely, arid, dead land!"

"Hm… Performance, ye say? Well, this town hasn't seen a performance since it was first founded. I'm sorry to say, but I don't think many of my townspeople would enjoy your music anyways. Us oldheads aren't into much of the newfangled electro-pop dizzy wizzy! Hehe…"

"For an elemental, you aren't much help. But thank you for the information."

Manny inquired, "Hm… I've heard that crocodile elementals are shapers of sand… That would explain why everything out here is made out of sand! Makim…

You're a crocodile, right? Maybe you could channel into

that real quick and make us a sturdy stage. Maybe even

a couple bleachers!"

"Ok, so one, I'm not a crocodile, I'm a GATOR, ok?!?

Two, I can't control anything right now, because Gators

only control ice! And this weather isn't exactly cold

weather friendly! Besides, I think I forgot how to kick

into my elemental powers… And thirdly, didn't you just

hear the man? What's the point in wasting our time

performing here when there's no one here!"

"He didn't say there was no one here, he just said no

one would show up. …Ok, so you got a point there.

Maybe we should've gone to Glandes Port City. I know if

we just walk far enough east we'll reach it. Hey Makim,

do you know where Naomi-" Manny froze, as the ground

abruptly began to shake.

Makim spotted a group of twelve or so Alligators

riding on motorbikes, rumbling towards the tiny village. Many

of the village people suddenly began running into their homes, and mothers desperately screamed for the few children that they had to come inside from playing. Most, that is.

They locked their doors in a cold sweat, leaving only few outside to fend for themselves, a fate they had chosen themselves. Amongst all the chaos Manny and Makim were very confused as to why these crocodiles would be so fearful. The gators arrived, and with them being so close Makim could see that all of their faces were smothered with olive green face paint. It seemed as though the moment the gators stepped foot in the town, it started drizzling, for the first time in decades.

Makim approached the group of gators, "Finally, some people we can ask for help! *Ahem,* Hello, fellow gators! My name is Makim, and my friend Manny and I just arrived in this small village town, expecting a much larger population to be here, but it seems that we might've landed on the wrong part of the map. Could you please kindly direct us to the nearest... shuttle bus, train... anything that can get us to Glandes Port City? No flights bring us there from this town..."

The head gator smiled bright, "Surprised to see one of our own people in a wretched place like this! It's so horrible that you had to be in a place like this."

"I know right? The heat here has been driving me crazy-"

"Oh! By the way, my name's Lilo. Those darn crocs. Did they do anything to hurt you or your friend?"

Makim hesitated, confused to be asked such a strange question, "Um... No? Why would any of the old folks out here harm anyone? They seem pretty kind-"

"You saw what one of these things did to my people?! They're murderers! They have no morals! They have no limits to what they'll do to hurt others! You must've seen. I've seen you performing with that tabby cat, the hero of Mai on TV, Naomi. You MUST'VE seen what happened that day! THEY are the reason for the release of Solituno!"

Lilo began lunging at the crocs that chose not to seek shelter. His men followed soon after, battering the gators with makeshift batons. Makim and Manny tried stopping them, but with no weapons and no plan, there was little they could do but to help the crocs get to shelter that had not already been attacked.

While Makim and Manny were stuck between a rock and a hard place, Naomi ventured off into the desert, following a seemingly never ending trail marked with large and shiny black and red painted rocks. To Naomi, it felt like days went by, but the sun hadn't moved a single inch since she started walking up a particularly large sand dune. She kept trekking, walking, tripping…falling… falling off a cliff?!?! Naomi fell down into an expansive ravine that was hidden within the top of the massive sand dune. She scrambled all she could but it was pointless, she was destined to fall to the depths of the desert.

The fall took a long time, about three minutes or so, and by the time Naomi reached the ground she already accepted her fate and was ready to embrace it, "*I've had a short run, but a short run is better than nothing at all, I guess.*"

But to her avail, there was a deep pond right in the

middle of the ravine. Naomi plunged into the water, and the splash was so loud, that by the time she got out of the pond, she could still hear the echoes of the water splashing. Naomi rested for a moment to regain her bearings, then realized the situation she was in.

She was possibly tens of miles deep within the earth, miles away from the nearest town, inside a… suspiciously well lit cave…? Naomi realized there were torches everywhere within the cave. Naomi caught a glimmer of shadow movement in one of the tunnels of the cave, and with that she caught a glimpse of hope - a chance to leave the cave and return to her friends.

Naomi chased the shadow on the walls of the cave hallway until she entered a small library, but as she already suspected, she was not alone. There were many short pebble-like creatures with googly eyes and large stone arms and legs. Naomi couldn't believe how something so small could thrive in such a cold and lonely place as a cave. They all froze, realizing someone was in their home.

"H-hello. My Name is Naomi. I come in peace, I'm just trying to leave..." She remembered the reason she left her friends in the first place, "Wait no- I've been told there's a place where I can learn more about Solituno. You know, the purple dragon with the deep raspy voice... scary looking...? Mean?"

The biggest stone creature emerged from the crowd of stones and spoke, "Why, hello there traveler! What far away lands do you come from?"

"I come from the west of Mai, by the coast."

"My oh my, such a long distance! Well, I heard you saying you'd like to hear more about Soituno, the embodiment of all that is bad?"

"Boy, this guy sure does go by a lot of names. But yes, please do tell me. I mean, I know where it came from, but is there anything about why Solituno keeps coming back?"

"Naomi, I assume Solituno has once again come, and once again been defeated?" Naomi nodded. "Naomi, nothing in this world can be literally created or destroyed. It is simply turned into something else.

Does water no longer exist once it evaporates? No! It simply turns a new, into another form, but only one that we cannot see. You see Naomi, every time Solituno has been, and hopefully, will be defeated, they don't disappear, but instead turn into another form of energy, this time to spread out to manifest in the physical world.

"But as it seems so, the world is growing ever hateful, and even within this isolated cave, I can feel it wont take nearly as long for Solituno to form back once again, if something is not done to heal our world. You cannot defeat Solituno, you simply stop them for the time being."

"I gotta sit cause you speak a whole lot *yawn*" Naomi sat down. "So you're telling me nothing can actually be destroyed or created, but changed to another form, yeah?"

"Yes, Naomi."

"So if that's the case, can't Solituno be turned good?"

"...I've never thought of that. I suppose so. But you'll need to know how to influence an individual like Solituno, and I have no answer for how to do that. I suppose Solituno themself would know, hehe... after all, they are the ones responsible for the birth of the crocodile race in Mai."

Naomi had nothing in her mouth, but if she did it would've been spit out everywhere, "So you're telling me, Solituno, the destruction guy, is the one who created the reptilian species? Like, so the old crocodile people way above from here were created by Solituno?"

"I thought I told you nothing can be created or destroyed! They weren't created by Solituno like sculptures formed from clay! They themselves were birthed from Solituno, and are blood related to Solituno. I would think this was common knowledge in the surface world! Or maybe outsiders don't know the rich history of this region of Mai..."

"That's crazy! So that means they got their sand powers

from Solituno, right?"

"No, elemental powers cannot be passed from birth,

but are given through means even I don't quite

comprehend ...I see something in you Naomi, I see

something I haven't ever seen in all of my thousands

of years of life... I see someone who is capable of

much more than they let themselves onto. I believe

you might just be capable of manipulating sand

through elemental power. Not just sand, I believe you

can control everything, the sea, the skies, rocks, fire,

lightning, you have potential, you just need to see it

within yourself!"

"...What are you talking about? I'm a Tabby, I have no

powers."

"Well then how were you able to defeat Solituno?"

"Well... let's see... Oh yeah! I started playing the drums and I passed out... Then I met Oritula Tali-"

"Oritula TALI?!? The spirit of hope? Joy? Determination? Never in all of my life have I ever seen such a vision. You must be special! Oh! Sorry for interrupting. Please, continue!"

"Yeah, so I met Oritula Tali in a vision I had after passing out, and Oritula Tali fused with me in some cool woozy form, then I came back, but with strength and power I had never felt before. I used that strength with the guidance of Oritula in my mind to beat the living cahoonies out of Solituno using my drum's sound wave emissions. And that's it really."

"For Oritula to have chosen you of all people to save Mai in its time of need, you must be of some importance. There's a way we could test to see if you're of the importance I believe you are."

The stone elder and Naomi strode back to the deep body of water in which Naomi dropped.

Naomi inquired, "So... What do I do now?"

"Elemental powers are primarily channeled through the outer extremities and torso. If you sit down, crisscross and meditate hard enough, you might be able to shape the stone in the cave to what it is you desire.

"But you have to think CAREFULLY! And hard on it too! If you let your mind get clouded, what you form might end up becoming your biggest problem. But focus on where you're trying to go too! Even too much positive thinking can be a deterrent from getting to where you need to be! You don't want to get stuck in a fairy tail and forget that you were trying to leave here in the first place!"

Naomi sat by the water in criss-cross and tried her best to focus. She wasn't much of a meditator, but she could concentrate when she truly put her mind to it. So she closed her eyes, and emptied her mind.

Naomi started hearing birds chirping and wind rustling her ears, contrasting the staleness of the air in the cave. Where was she? She opened her eyes and was astounded by the sight. She had woken up sitting across from a large staircase, which she couldn't see the end of. Naomi felt oddly calm despite the strange scenario, and proceeded to walk up the stairs. She felt, for some reason, that she would find something if she walked long enough.

Naomi continued to walk up the steps for what seemed like hours until she finally arrived at a large field of rock and sand. In the midst of the rubble was a big stone emblem, shining, almost as if tho it were purposely making itself noticeable to Naomi.

She ran to the stone emblem and tried to pick it up, but it felt like it was superglued to the floor. She spent a full hour trying ways to get the emblem off the floor. Kicking it, pulling it, all of the above. Just as Naomi was ready to call it quits and find another way out, the emblem grew into a stone giant, ten floors in height and weighing well over a couple hundred tons.

The giant introduced itself, "I am Audax, ruler of the earth and protector of the earth emblem. Who may you mere mortal be, that you feel so privileged to even attempt to take this precious tool?"

"Hello, I'm Naomi. I come from another... well, universe I guess... I don't really know where I am, but I really feel like that emblem would help me get to where I need to be."

"Naomi, what quest are you on that has led you to believe you are worthy of the stone emblem?"

"Hehe... Long story short, I need to get back to my friends, and the only way I'll be able to get to them is if I master the element of earth."

Suddenly, Audax became furious, "Just who do you think you are?!? You are not of any capability to learn any elemental power, most definitely not of the earth! You are a TABBY! You have no power nor potential. For you to disrespect the worth of the emblem means a certain death for you!"

Audax chased Naomi, not for long though before

Naomi was trapped in a corner of the sky high rock and sand platform. Audax started sliding Naomi closer and closer to the cliff, but surprisingly enough, despite its large size and strength, Naomi stood mostly firm. But not for long. Inches became feet, feet yards until Naomi was on the near edge of the platform.

Naomi contemplated her next move, *"How do I get out of this!?! AHH how'd I get in this place to begin with? Oh yeah! Meditation!"*

Naomi ran to the very edge of the platform and sat down, closed her eyes and ignored everything around her. The possibility she might not get the earth emblem, didn't matter to her. The possibility of her getting pushed off the edge of the platform, didn't matter to her at this moment. The possibility she might not ever find a way out of this place, did not matter.

Audax was wiping its hand across the platform, targeting Naomi, intending to send her flying. Then, his hand swatted her. But Naomi didn't move a single inch. It was almost as if Naomi herself had turned into stone, the strongest of all stone. She was still, unmoving and unbothered by the problems around her. Naomi realized this was her chance. She jumped on Audax's hand, ran upwards at lighting speed and punched the heart of Audax, that being the earth emblem, with all of her might. Then, the giant fell, to the fury of a little, but now more powerful than ever, tabby cat.

"GHAGH! Okay, okay! You have proven yourself worthy of the emblem. This was but a test to see if you were truly worthy. Here, take it."

"Yeah right! What would've happened if I failed the test? I would've been flying off to who knows where, and you know it!"

"Hohoho! Naomi, I want you to know the significance of this emblem, its true importance and its role in the creation of everything in the physical world. When you wake up, this emblem will not be with you, but you will know the many secrets that it holds, and you will be able to morph the earth to your own desire. I do say to you, do not ever use the emblem to commit evil, for good cannot mix with bad, and good that is used for bad will eventually be of no use."

"Uh... Can you speak in normal people's terms?"

"*Sigh*, don't use your new powers for bad, or you might lose them. And who knows if they'll come back!"

Naomi nodded and grabbed the emblem, and when she did, sparks of light began to jolt all around her, until everything went black. Then she woke from her meditation, and time seemingly had not changed since she had left the physical world. Naomi used her newfound powers to create a small pillar underneath her feet, and she raised it like an elevator, eager to return to her friends and show them her new powers.

Makim and Manny were in a wee bit of trouble, as Lilo and his gang of gators had left, but the condition the citizens were left in, was unfavorable. Many had their jewelry and clothing stolen, and food destroyed. Some were beaten, some had permanent injuries, like broken spines and dented skulls, bashed in from what the gators had done to them.

Makim and Manny tried their best to provide comfort

to the citizens, and the ones who had stayed inside did as well, but with no form of transportation or communication, they were left on their own. That is, until Makim spotted a large wave of sand coming straight at them. It seemed things were going to get worse.

"First we find ourselves in this old rusty village, then the old rusty village gets pillaged, and now what?? We're going to be drowned in sand?"

Manny looked closer at the tsunami, and saw a familiar tabby surfing on top of it. "Makim, we're not going to drown, that's Naomi!"

"Oh, now I see her! Typical Naomi... WAIT, WHAT?! How is she surfing the sand?"

Naomi entered the village, quelled the wave she had formed, and jumped down. The village's new look was much to her dismay, and both sides had questions to ask, and answers to give.

"Eh, eh...? You like my cool new powers? Wait no! Let me ask you this first... WHAT HAPPENED TO THIS PLACE?!?"

"Well, ya see... uhh... Makim, I think I've suddenly

forgotten, could you care to explain?"

"Really, Manny? Alright. Naomi, ya see, this gator guy named Lilo and a little short of a baker's dozen more gators showed up. I tried introducing myself, and they just started talking crazy about the people here, talking all 'Oh those darn crocs are to blame for everything' then just started ransacking the place! They started attacking people, but there's not much Manny and I could do against like, over a dozen gators, so we could only try to help them get to safety. Then they just up and left, northwards."

Naomi stood frozen, wondering why anyone would commit such heinous acts. Then it clicked in her head, "Guys, guys! I think I might know why that uh... Lilo, I think? Well whatever it was, I think I know why they'd think they are responsible for the Solituno attack!"

"What excuse could they possibly have to do something like this?"

"Now, hear me out... I know I'm going to sound pretty crazy, but... the entirety of the crocodile race came directly from

SOLITUNO."

"Hah! Now, I don't know where you got those powers from, but clearly they came with some side effects."

"No, I'm being serious! Why would I be joking at a time like this?"

"Naomi, you'd joke at the most inappropriate times."

"Okay, but I'm being serious, trust me! You see, I fell down this big ravine in the middle of the desert, and ran deep into a cave system, met this group of stone people, asked them about Solituno and the leader told me all about them, and told me that the crocs came from Solituno. Then the leader told me that I had all sorts of powers, and that I just needed to unlock them. They told me to meditate and I did. Then I like, got transported to a whole other universe or something and I had to battle this big rock guardian, and it called itself Audax, and ya know what? I beat it! Next thing you know, I'm lifting myself out of the ravine with a rock platform, then I surf the smooth sand waves of the desert back to you guys."

"You know what, I'll take your word. But chances are those gators will come back, so what do we do now Naomi?"

"Okay so one, for some reason now we're some sort of crew of superheroes now, just going around saving the day and whatnot? Who said we had to fix all this? And two, When did I become the one with all the answers? I don't know how to stop them!" Then, once more, It clicked for Naomi, "Ohh, I got an idea guys! Back when I was battling Solituno, I met this other person.. Their name was Oritula."

"And... When was this? When did you have time to meet Oritula??"

"Enough with asking questions, Makim. Anyways, they told me that Solituno was formed once again as a result of all of the... negative energy in Tamiba City?"

"Makes sense."

"Makim, hush."

"Okay, okay. I'll wait till you finish talking."

"As I was saying, if we convince the gators that the crocs

aren't the reason for the reemergence of Solituno, maybe they'll chill off! Makim, you may speak."

"Good Idea, but how do we go through with it? They went way north, and Glandes Port City is the only place I know north from here. You know how long it's gonna take for us to get to the GPC on foot? Too long!"

Naomi thought for a moment. Then, it clicked. Hey…what's going on with all this clicking? Naomi falls down a ravine and gets some powers and all of a sudden her brain works faster than ever. Anyways, Naomi realized the potential her new powers held, and she used them to her advantage. She morphed a large clump of the ground into a dirt and sand suit, and it looked just like her! She channeled her elemental power to form a staircase and Makim and Manny could tell what was going to happen next. They plopped themselves onto seats on the suit's shoulders, and Naomi went into the control panel in the suit's chest cavity. Then the old crocodile Makim talked to expressed his concerns for his community.

"Oh, young fellers, I do hope you come back

soon with that suit! We could use some
protection around here, and my powers
aren't as strong as they were a couple
decades ago."

"Don't worry sir! When we finish up our mission, you won't
be needing this suit!"

The desert is not a lovely place. It has no mercy on
those who don't prepare for its inferno fueled wrath. But
Naomi and the gang were moving at race car speeds thanks to
Naomi's suit. Her earth powers ran on her willpower to carry
on, to stay bold and grounded despite the strong winds that
may come her way.

Within what seemed like no time the gang arrived on
the outer brink of Glandes Port City. Naomi waited for Makim
and Manny to leave the suit, then she jumped out and she let it
collapse back into the earth. They were met with a surprisingly
warm welcome by the city guards.

"Welcome to Glandes Port City! The city of the seas!"
The crew wasted no time entering the city, but one was deeply

regretful of entering.

"Ghagh! It smells horrible here! *hack hack* GARLIC! Let's hurry up and find those guys, there must be some place where we can find them. Like... A motorcycle club or something! "

Naomi soon found a batch of mint cloves in a patch of grass, smashed them with a rock and smeared it on her upper lip and neck. But she still wanted to hurry up, because the soothing scent of mint was sure to be overrun by a rotten fragrance, one even worse than garlic.

The crew continued exploring the land of Glandes Port City, and once Naomi became adjusted to the mixed scent of mint and garlic she began to truly marvel at the sight. The sea was within eye view, and the hot sun glimmered on the dark cyan waters of Glandes Port City. The city was big. A little overwhelming from the perspective of Naomi, because of how few people there seemed to be in the city. Most, if not all of the people in the city were gators, and they were wearing military attire. A particularly passive looking gator walked by and smiled at the crew.

Naomi felt it was time she got some information on what was going on, "Hey there! You see, me and my friends just arrived here in the GPC to uh... admire the astounding waters! And we were just wondering why there's like, no one here? I mean this is a pretty big city, why aren't there people to fill it up?"

"Hello travelers! The answer to that question is quite simple. Everyone left! They saw the opportunity and fortune that Tamiba City offered and they ran for it. But that's not the only reason. Ever since those Calidum `City' crocs came trying to integrate into our beloved home, no one could stand the possibility of living with the direct descendant of Solituno! I'm sure you know. You defeated Solituno after all."

Makim and Manny knew what Naomi had told them, but they were both stunned to hear another person tell them the crocodilian race came from Solituno. Naomi was furious to hear the hatred of the gators being expressed through this guard, whom she believed was very ignorant. But she resisted yelling out and stayed composed to get more answers.

"Hm... Interesting. Well, why are you in all of this military attire? Is this GPC culture or something?"

"Haha! You've got a sense of humor, I appreciate that. The few gators that stayed true to this city and did not flee to Tamiba city valiantly.. Let's just say, they got rid of the crocs that tried moving here. Too many of them came here. It was a big operation, too big for us to complete efficiently. Unfortunately some did escape, and they went back to their shabby little excuse of a community. Now, we're just about ready to finish the job and take the rest out. I'm just waiting for the boss's orders tomorrow, to swipe the last of them."

The gang's hearts dropped in unison, feeling the weight of what had happened in the city they stood in just days ago. How such a heinous operation could be pulled off, in such a short period of time was beyond their comprehension. Knowing the lengths these people would go to in order to seek vengeance on others, they all wanted to leave as soon as possible. Makim, being a gator himself, felt if he tried convincing the gator that crocs were not responsible for

Solituno's emergence, they'd listen, so he ushered Naomi to recall her interaction with Oritula.

"So, I'm the gal who defeated Solituno, yeah? And guess what? I know why they formed again in the first place. It's not because of the crocs, they have virtually nothing to do with it."

"What are you talking about? What nonsense are you speaking? There's no other possibility other than the crocs wanting to… well I'm not sure but I just know they wanted to bring Solituno back for some reason!"

"Wait, just let me speak! *Sigh* Right before I started going all power crazy and shattered Solituno, I kind of passed out, and when I did I was in this big white void, and Oritula was there. I'm sure you know her right? The good guy, yeah? Well anyways, she told me that Solituno draws strength from negative energy, and that she drew strength from positive energy. She herself said that Solituno came back because of the collective negative energy concentrated within Tamiba City! Not even all of the crocs are at fault because so many other races live there!"

"Yeah right. Like I'd believe that. Why would Oritula want to talk to you specifically anyways?"

"Oritula told me she saw my determination - my willpower, she saw what I was made of and she liked it. She knew I was the one that would be able to save not only Tamiba City, but all of Mai."

"Well even if you ARE telling the truth, no one's going to believe you here. Besides, we might as well finish off what we started, regardless of whether or not we're right."

It was clear that there was no turning back. There was going to be a battle amongst the two nations, and only one side would win. Naomi had one final question to ask before they fled the scene, "Well, let me ask you this, and then we'll leave. Who's this leader's name that you spoke of earlier?"

"Our leader has the title of General of the GPC militia, and they go by General Lilo."

It was clear now that there was no peaceful resolution to this conflict. Makim was enraged, his fists clenched, he was so upset that if it were not so arid in the desert on the way back to Calidum City, he would have been steaming.

"I can't believe those people! What kind of people would try to decimate an entire population of people because of something that happened halfway across the world that they couldn't even control?!? My own people?!?"

"Makim, I know you're mad. Trust, we all are. But just know you are absolutely nothing like those people back there. If anything, you're the one good thing that's come out of that place."

"Thank you Naomi. I needed that. But we still need to prepare everyone that's able to fight for war. There's no way of knowing what's to come for tomorrow. As far as we know, this could not only be the crocs, but our last stand as well. So if it is, we need to be prepared."

There was no time to waste. To start off, Manny counted the total population of Caldum City aged 18 - 50 that would be able to engage in combat. Only 63. Then, everyone collectively gathered whatever supplies and natural resources they had to build makeshift weapons. They made spears, bows and arrows, crossbows, slingshots - whatever they could build with what little they had.

They killed off the last of their cattle to create leather armor. They believed they would not need to worry about starving, as they believed it was very unlikely anyone would live through what was to come.

Secondly, Makim trained everyone for close combat. Makim was not only a bassist and culinary master, but also knowledgeable in the art of offensive attacking. He knew how to use a variety of weapons as well.

He had everyone that was fit enough go through a series of physical tests to test their speed, stamina, reaction time, and strength. It was clear that strength alone would not win this battle, but strategic movements to take out the most men with what little of a makeshift last stand militia they had formed. There was retaliation though, as some wanted to abandon their home. But Makim kept them loyal through his skillful use of the edible plants and fowls wandering the city to make lunch. Some even said his cooking was to die for.

After this, Naomi divided the militia into three groups, between herself, Makim and Manny. Manny would lead 26 crocs, them being the best fit to use spears, bows and crossbows. He named them the Stealth Squad. Makim would lead another 26 crocs, with spears built for close combat action, and swordsmen, most of them having the fastest hands and reaction time. He named them the Front Squad.

Naomi gave herself the last 11 members, which Makim claimed were the best of the litter. Naomi would lead an elite force of crocs, the fastest on their feet, and stealthy as well. Since the desert wasn't completely flat, they would have no problem sneaking up on gators clueless to what they were planning. She named them the Surprise Squad. Makim and Manny's groups had just enough leather armor for protection, but Naomi's had none. Naomi already saw this coming, and so she channeled her elemental energy to form the strongest, impenetrable armor formed from the hardest of rocks and minerals. The armor was surprisingly comfortable, as Naomi was able to make them custom sized.

They made a plan, recited it to the members of the militia and they prepared a feast with the dead cattle used for leather, but not so much that the militia would become sluggish or struggle to sleep. There were murmurs of the possibility that the battle might last longer than one day, so they decided to hide barrels of smoked cattle meat in pits, and covered them in sand, hiding it all under a specified home. The elderly, young and disabled were all brought far away from Calidum City, further south, to live in the airport, as refugees for the time being, and in case all went wrong, they were provided with enough money to buy airport food and fly back to Tamiba City, as this was the only flight the airport provided. The sun set, and they all ate an herb that only grew in the Seascape desert of Mai, called peace leaves, which calmed their nerves and allowed them to sleep peacefully.

Morning arrived all too soon for everyone. A heavy

fog of doubt had fallen over much of the militia, but they knew they truly had no choice at this point. Makim went over the battle plan once more to freshen everyone's memory.

"Alright, come along everyone, let's revise this one more time. So first, positions. The Gators are expected to be coming from the north, so my squad, and I will be in three groups of nine, not too far from each other, all facing north. My squad is best for quick close combat action, we'll be able to beat the ground battle if we stay coordinated. We'll be in the center."

One of the members of the Front Squad expressed their determination, "Knowing what we're fighting for, and knowing there is no other option, we will fight as furiously as we can, because if we lose, all will be lost."

"I'm sorry this is happening to you. I appreciate your determined spirit. And Manny, let's go over your position."

"Right. *ahem* Alright, so my squad, that being the Stealth Squad, will be on the ends of the horizontal facing line the Front Squad will be in. I will be leading one end, made of 12 members, while the other, made of 13 members, will be led by the highest performing member in my squad. His name is Nexal. Nexal, come up here."

"Hello. I would say that it is a pleasure to be leading into war, but considering the circumstances we're in, I'd say this is not a pleasure, but an obligation."

 "Thank you, Nexal. We will both use our long range weapons to destroy as many motorbikes as we can, and attack them from the sides, while being far enough to not immediately be targeted, as we only have daggers for close range weapons. And Naomi, let's revise your plan."

Naomi got caught in a daydream, then popped out of her haze, "Alright, my eleven elite fighters, that I named the Surprise Squad, will stay hidden for the first portion of the battle, until either most of the gator militia comes close enough to become encircled, or the other squads need help. Regardless, when we do come out, my squad and I will be in virtually impenetrable armor, crafted by me, and come out with my secret weapon - really long, sharp swords made of obsidian, and serrated with sand attached to our armor. My elite force will be quick and stealthy in this heavy armor and we'll sneak up on them from behind and go haywire, and leave no olive green gator standing! Then, if we've won, we call the elderly, young and disabled back, we take the gator's supplies and we leave you all to rebuild."

"Olive green gator? Huh?"

"Didn't you see, Makim? Everyone we ran into in the GPC had olive green face paint on. That's how we'll know when it's time for battle. When we see a large, sickeningly dull olive green blob of movement marching our way."

"So I think we all have the plan in our heads now. If this is to go wrong though, I want you all to know, I've had a blast spending my time with you all"

"Yeah, I feel the same way."

"Yeah, we all do."

The blob of olive green wretchedness had made its

way above the horizon. Everyone got into their positions,
prepared for whatever was to happen. The numbers weren't
even, but they were numbers they could work with. There
were 63 Calidum City militia members to around 191 Glandes
Port City militia members. Over trice the size of the Calidum
City militia. This, was Calidum's last stand.

The GPC militia charged at high speeds, with
motorbikes following them behind. As expected, they all
attacked towards the middle. Though the numbers were not in
their favor, the Front Squad stayed grounded, and fought
fiercely, and this came as a big surprise to the gators, who
believed they had not even formed a resistance to combat their
arrival.

The Stealth Squad took out a number of motorbikes,
most killing their riders as well, because they were going at
such high speeds in an attempt to take down the Calidum City
forces they would get sent flying or dragged across the
ground, tearing up their armor and leading to their death.

They were stunned by the skill the crocodiles had, but
the GPC militia pushed harder and the Front Squad folded,

and began pulling back. The GPC militia began running frantically in it's significantly larger numbers to follow the much faster Front Squad, and in the panic some GPC militia began running and trampling over each other, and with all this confusion the Surprise Squad popped around behind the GPC militia and closed them in, and the Stealth Squad did so as well. The Surprise squad began the true massacre.

These highly trained 11 members used all of their energy to swing their blades at every gator coming their way. Soon enough, the last gator was taken out, and there layed a sea of lifeless gators, a pile of scaly blood stained shirts.

It took days to drag all of the dead GPC militia out of Calidum City and bury them. It was clear that Calidum City was going to need to be reestablished, and start anew. When the battle mindset was quelled, everyone was both astounded and fearful of what they had done. But that fear soon fell null when they recalled the atrocities that took place that led to this battle in the first place.

They were not aggressors, they had simply defended

themselves. There was no need to feel bad for what they had done. They fought against their oppressors and won.

Around this time the gang was ready to get out of the entirety of the Seascape area. They said their goodbyes, and headed off for the airport. Until they realized they had no money to fly back. How unfortunate.

"Guys, I'm not sure how we're going to get out of this place…"

"See? I told you guys coming here was a bad idea! That heat drives everyone crazy and look - look at what we've done! We've led a whole army into battle!"

"Militia."

"Alright, militia. Since when did you become the queen of proper vocabulary usage?"

"Don't give me such a title! Manny, I think we should just leave our equipment here, take our backpacks and head… literally any other direction than directly up north. Then, we could sort of… travel around Mai, living off the land and whatnot."

"Naomi, we're musicians, not adventurers. I say we

wait here and just hope someone comes over here and finds us!”

“Makim, I'm really starting to think about using your hard head as a snare drum. Yeah, we're musicians. But now, after what we've done for the people here, we are vigilantes too. Besides, I feel like this earth power I have isn't the only power I'm able to use... I just need to find the rest!”

“Yeah, you've got a point Naomi. Besides, it will be fun to explore Mai! We live in a really expansive land. Even a whole lifetime might not be enough to explore every nook and cranny!”

“*Sigh* Alright, fine. But just know, if anything goes wrong, I won't say it, but just know I told you guys so. But how will we decide where we will go?”

“Easy, we do a three sided dice toss. Since straight north is out of the picture, one would be west, two north east so we don't run into the coast, and three south.”

“Ok, but who here has a three sided dice? Matter of fact I didn't even know that existed.”

Naomi pulled a three sided dice out of her pocket and rolled it on the ground. It landed on two.

“North east, it is!”

It was decided. Our three vigilantes would be going north east for their next adventure. What may they find? What new environments will they undergo? In time, we will certainly know.

Ⅲ

Naomi, the Elemental of Mai

It was a wonderful day in the land of Mai. Birds were chirping, the sun was gleaming… And our three heroes have finally escaped from the desert! But, where were they now…? Well, let's just say, they may have left the desert, but they most certainly have not left the heat! What they ventured into was a landscape full of volcanoes and riddled with molten lava lakes.

"OH COME ON" Makim whined.

"How does a place like this even exist in real life?!? This looks like it's straight out of a nightmare!"

"Well, you chose to go north east, Naomi…"

"I DIDN'T CHOOSE THIS PLACE, IT WAS THE DICE!"

"Now, I'm not going back to that desert village, so riddle me this Naomi… How exactly does one cross a landscape such as this, huh?"

"Simple, Makim. We walk, but as far away from the lava as we can! I'm sure we'll find a better place if we just march on through this place!"

With that being said, the three began their trek across the molten volcano landscape. The sky soon turned a thick dark gray as ashes began filling up the sky, but they kept moving. It wasn't all that long until they ran into a very peculiar looking creature, which had appeared from the corner of a boulder. It was seemingly made of… fire? Well, at least somewhat resembling a small fox, made of fire.

It seemed intrigued by the gang and spoke, "*Why, hello there travelers! What brings you here, in the Land of Embers?*"

"Hello! My name is Naomi, and these are my friends Makim and Manny. We're on an adventure throughout the land of Mai, having just left the desert region after a… Well, let's just say we solved a conflict, and now we're here."

"*Well, I know your name of course! I saw you on TV, Naomi! Oh- how rude of me! I forgot to introduce myself! My name is Combustal, and I am the chief of this land, the Land of Embers! If you'd like, I could bring you to one of my towns, Inferna Town! You could try this region's famous hot foods! Plus, It'd give you a place to rest before you continue on with your journey."*

"Now that's what I'm talking about! Sign me up!"

The crew followed Chief Combustal for a mile or so until they finally reached Inferna Town. The scenery of the city was beautiful, though it nearly blended in with the environment. The building walls and roofs were coal black, and lamp posts burned bright red, cutting through the muddy gray sky. Many other wolf-like creatures were outside as well playing games, eating and attempting to sell various items to each other. It seemed quite lively. It was surprising to Naomi that these creatures were able to thrive in such an unforgiving environment.

"That sky never seems to clear up, huh?"

"Hah, never! That's just the way it is here. The high volcanic activity never gives the sky a chance to turn blue. Lots of ash clouds stay here."

Chief Combustal then led Naomi into a tavern, and told Makim and Manny to stay outside, and explore the area.

The tavern was filled with all sorts of old crackled papers and incense.

"So... why'd you bring me here again?"

"I feel it in my bones. Yes, you must be an elemental master of sorts. What element do you possess?"

"Uh- well, I can move around sand and dirt... earth. I control the elements of earth."

"Aha, I knew it! Well, you may have the element of earth, but do you possess the element of fire?"

"Uhhh. No, I can't. Why do you ask?"

"There is an ancient prophecy, as old as time as we know it, that has been passed down in the Land of Embers. It claims that there will be two more reemergences of Solituno Tali, the devourer of peace, both of which end in its defeat."

"Well, I defeated Solituno for the second time, heh. Hopefully a third time doesn't happen though..."

"Oh! Let me further explain in the form of a smoke story..."

Combustal then picked up a large orange and gold striped incense, then lit it, waving its smoke all around Naomi's face.

"Uh what's that?"

"Shhh, don't worry, just wait, and you'll see. The smoke of this incense will make you significantly more immersed into the story in which I'm telling you. You will see the story with your own eyes."

The smoke stung Naomi's eyes, but they soon adjusted. She started seeing an array of flashing colors and shapes.

"Now, as I was saying... Oh yes, you, Naomi, have defeated Solituno in its second coming, and the prophecy says that you, the defeater of Solituno in its second coming, will be the one to defeat Solituno once and for all... though Solituno will be unfathomably stronger the next, and last time you encounter it."

"Ok, so one - great, Solituno's coming back, yeah, kinda felt like that was gonna happen. Two, how do I defeat it once and for all, if it's supposed to be a kajillion times stronger

than what it ALREADY IS?"

"Don't worry, listen to the tale of the prophecy. It is

also said that you won't be alone on this journey

either. It is said that you will need help from

companions to achieve forms of higher levels of

power, wisdom and energy to defeat Solituno Tali.

Your elemental power, yes? Well, unlike everyone

else in the land of Mai, you are able to possess not

only more than one element, but every single one.

Not only are you able to, but it's more so of a

requirement. To gain the higher level you need in

order to be able to defeat Solituno, you will have to

continue traveling the land of Mai. In time, you will

be brought to where you can become a master of

each element. Naomi, you are special, you will fulfill

this prophecy and thus, your destiny."

The smoke then cleared, and Naomi was brought back into the waking world of smokey air and ancient scrolls piled on top of one another.

"I already knew I was special, but this is kind of.. Well, just confirmation of what I already knew! Hehe!"

Combustal could feel Naomi's uncertainty, her uncertainty of whether she would be able to defeat Solituno once more, *"How about we come back out to find your friends, Naomi?"*

"Yeah, I'd like that."

While Naomi and Combustal were busy dealing with world fate level prophecies, Makim and Manny decided to talk to the locals of Inferna Town about what exactly there was to do.

Makim came across a shop full of weapons, but one that really caught his eye was a large, gold plated sword with blue sapphires encrusted on the handle bars. Why the town even had a weapon shop, was not clear. These fox-like creatures didn't seem like the type of creatures that could engage in close combat, at least to Makim. He went in to ask about the sword.

"Hello there, umm ya see, I just happened to see that stunning golden sword over there, and I'd like to know how much it costs."

"600 bucks, mate! Would you like it?"

Makim's eyes widened at the price, "Erm- no thanks. Actually, I'll just be on my way."

Just as Makim was halfway out of the door, the shopkeeper called him back, **"Wait a minute now! Let me make a deal with you."**

"I'm listening..."

"You see, we've recently been having this little problem here in Inferna. On the outskirts of town, there's this mountain with blue lava inside it. We call it Moquteal's Mt. People love to visit every year around this time, when it's least active, but recently there's been some sort of... creature? Something, that's scaring our townsfolk from going up to Moquteal's Mt!"

"Nice. Now what does this have to do with me and the sword?"

"Well, if you go up there and deal with whatever's scaring people away from the mountain, you can take the sword with you. And if you come back alive, you can keep it."

Makim thought about the deal for a moment, then picked up the sword. It was shockingly lightweight for such a large weapon.

"Hey, don't worry man! Me and my crew will deal with whatever's up there."

"Thank you, kind sir! You can't miss the mountain, it's the biggest one here, and it's really nice, and blue... oh, and there's cracks with blue lava oozing out of it!"

Makim left the shop with his brand new sword and quickly found Manny, who was kicking his feet in a small pile of ashes.

"Hey! Manny, look! You see anything new about me?"

Makim brought attention to his back, where he had put the sword in a casing. Manny wasn't as impressed as he expected.

"Let me guess. You stole it."

"Wha...? No, I made a deal."

"And what exactly was that deal?"

"Yeah Makim, what deal?"

Makim jumped, and turned around to see Naomi, with Combustal, returning from their prophetic storytelling.

"Ok guys, so there's this mountain called Moquteal's Mt. It's blue and it's the biggest one, you can see it from here. People here love to go up to that mountain, but apparently there's something up there scaring them from going the whole way up. So I say let's go up there and help these people so they can once again enjoy their mountain!"

"You just want the sword."

"Well that too, but, how about it?"

"I'm in. What about you, Naomi?"

"Yeah, sure, let's go!"

The team arrived at the base of the mountain, and began trekking up the mountain trail. The sky had seemingly, out of nowhere, turned a deep dark burgundy. The ground on the trail was covered in a thick deep brown haze, but it only went up to their ankles. It was sticky on the ground, almost as if there was syrup laid all around the area.

They walked for quite some time, they climbed for some time, and they were gonna sleep for some time as well, as the night came. It was already dim in the Land of Embers, but even they could tell, it was getting even darker.

They searched for a safe place to rest, not for long though, until they ran into a small cave. I bet you'd think it was hard for them to sleep, considering they might be crept on by whatever they're trekking up the mountain to encounter, yet they all slept quite well. Maybe it was the fumes.

Naomi woke up to the sound of a loud grumble in the ground, her eyes immediately laid upon a small river way over in the distance. Wait - no - it was lava! Blue lava. The ground suddenly started grumbling again, even more aggressively, and Makim and Manny awoke.

"Is the volcano erupting?!?"

"No Makim, I don't think so. I mean..."

"Don't think so?"

"I don't know. I mean this is the second time it happened, so..."

"I think we should stop debating if it's gonna erupt and hurry up with this mission, so if it DOES, we're not here bickering."

"Yeah yeah, fine."

With being encouraged by the elements, the team started pacing up the mountain a bit faster. Then another grumble came, then another, then one that was so loud and disruptive they had to sit down until it passed because it would've made them fall.

They started running, starting to become quite sure the mountain would erupt, the only undetermined factor being, when, it would erupt. Hopefully not until they came back down. They soon made it to the top of the mountain, which was quite large and surprisingly flat. The dark gray clouds were so close it seemed they could touch them if they jumped high enough. They moved much faster than they seemed to move from the ground. It was intimidating almost, seeing how high they were. Quite a marvel.

But amongst all this adventuring they had not seen a single creature, and they didn't see anything up at the top. So where was this supposed enemy?

"I'm so glad we wasted a day and a half of our time climbing up a volcanic mountain! I just know it's gonna get really good when we all get submerged in lava when it erupts!"

"Shut up Makim. You were part of this idea!"

Makim mumbled something back, but it wasn't coherent. Naomi, getting a funny feeling, decided to take a look in the mouth of the volcano. What she saw was a marvelous, blue phoenix. It looked up at Naomi, and flapped its wings to come to her. Makim and Manny soon saw the large bird in the sky and jumped in fear.

"You're telling me we're supposed to defeat THIS thing?"

"Hehe... well maybe 'defeat' is the wrong choice of words. Maybe we could survive this thing."

"MAKIM, IT'S COMING TOWARDS ME, HELP!"

Makim ran to Naomi and pulled out his sword, unsure if it would do any good against the behemoth of a bird that laid before them. But to their surprise, the bird flew right up to Naomi, and started speaking.

"You are Naomi, the supposed hero of Mai, yes?"

"Uh.. yeah?"

"The prophecies must be true then."

"...Huhhh??"

"I am the last elemental fire master of Mai, Phontrix. I have waited a long time for your arrival. It was instructed to me that I give you the secrets of the element of fire, so that you may become a fire master."

Naomi stood confused for a moment, but soon started asking questions, "You want to help me? Well I have a question for you first. Have you been scaring people away from this mountain?"

"Yes."

"Why?!"

"I was told to protect this mountain until Naomi, the prophesied hero of Mai, comes."

"Who's bossing you around like this, huh?"

"That is not of your concern. Now, to become a master of fire, you must become one with the element. Embody bravery!"

"How exactly do I do that?"

"Simply touch my beak."

"But aren't you like, a kajillion degrees? Won't that like, burn me?"

"Be brave, Naomi. It might, might not. But whether it does or not, you have to be brave!"

"Naomi, not gonna lie, this seems like a bad idea-"

"Silence! Do not interfere with this."

"Oop-"

Naomi was initially hesitant, but realized soon that this was the only way she could gain the element of fire. Phontrix was the last master of fire in Mai. So she walked up to the phoenix, held her hand out, and slapped her palm on its beak.

The heat was painful. Really painful. The bird

opened its eyes wide as ever and began shooting fire in an

array of colors. Red, orange, blue, green, black… Every last

bit of wisdom it had of the fire element, into Naomi. Naomi

saw all of this information through flashes of visions, and in

the last vision, there was an emblem, on fire. She remembered

the emblem she saw in her haze in the ravine of the desert.

"Hey… I've seen one of you before!"

Naomi snatched the emblem and put it around her

neck. Then the visions stopped, and the bird stepped back.

Naomi looked around. She was still in the Land of Embers.

She looked at her palm. It had a mark on it, shaped like a fire.

But it didn't hurt. The emblem was no longer on her neck. Her

eyes bursted into golden flames, then shunned back into her.

Makim and Manny marveled at the sight.

"So, Naomi, are you now a master of fire?"

Naomi swiped her hand into the air, with intent to

release fire, then a fireball bursted out. She kicked her feet up,

and fire bursted out. She now possessed the element of fire.

"Yeah, I guess I am."

The phoenix nodded, then flew away, and as it flew away, the sky in the Land of Embers cleared for the first time in forever.

In the aftermath of it all, the gang were paid handsomely for "fending off" Phontrix with a big bag of coffles, a rare metal. Black, high in value, and low in weight. Inferna Town held a large celebratory parade to celebrate the phoenix's departure. Long lines of upright wolves held flags and walked around, playing songs of joy.

The surrounding crowd was cheerful, and the overall mood was bright, and it lasted all through the dark night. Naomi went back to the foot Moquteal's Mt. She stood for a while, wondering what would happen next. Makim and Manny followed her up, though she didn't know.

Makim slapped Naomi on the back, "Ayyy Naomi, how's it going?"

"Ah! Oh, Makim. I'm good."

Manny sat down with her, "What's up Naomi? We know something's up. Tell us."

"Well if you really want to know... I have earth powers, and now I have fire."

Naomi lifted her hand up and sparked a flame to illuminate their surroundings.

"But what's next? What do I do now? I'm just confused about the road ahead of us, that's all."

"Well, I guess all we can do now is try to find a way out of the Land of Embers. I only know a bit of the desert region, but Mai is so big and all, so I'm sure there's some other bird guy waiting for you or something."

"Yeah, things always seem to work out for us Naomi. Makim, that sounds like a good idea."

The next day, the gang said their goodbyes to Chief Combustal, and went on their way. Don't worry, I'm sure they'll end up just about where they've ought to be.

IV

Fear no Illusions

You remember what happened the last time you

were here, right? Well, let me fill you in, just in case you

forgot. Naomi, the hero of Mai and her mates Makim and

Manny escaped the desert region and entered into a volcanic

land of fire and, more than that, surprises! A Sphinx was

terrorizing the local creatures who went up the biggest

volcanic mountain in the region, Moquteal's Mt.

Naomi and her gang went to the Sphinx, and there

was no real battle, but a discussion of Naomi's destiny, for this

Sphinx was placed by… destiny? Well, it was there that

Naomi discovered the true potential she could reach, that earth

was not the only element she was capable of mastering, but

fire as well. And all of the other elements that were in Mai.

And now, here we are, in the present day! What wondrous

world will our superb heroes enter into next? Well, let's see...

The gang continued their travel through the Land of

Embers, and as they continued walking, the sky began

spewing volcanic ash more and more frequently, and

aggressively, until the ash pour became so much that they couldn't see what was right in front of them.

"Guys?! Where are you? Can you hear me?"

"Yeah, I can hear you just fine. Let's just keep walking."

The three held hands so they wouldn't lose track of one another. Surprisingly enough, there were no trips nor stumbles in their period of blind walking, but what was even more surprising, was the sight they saw when the ash suddenly vanished, revealing a polar opposite environment to where they were before. A forest, at sunset, with thick tall willow trees with light blue leaves, covered in frost from the cold. The ground was relatively flat, and covered in a thin layer of snow.

"Uhh. Guys, if I remember right, we were just in the Land of Embers, yeah?"

"Yeah.. hm. Well maybe we've been walking for longer than we thought through the ash."

"Makim, clearly we didn't walk far enough to walk into the polar opposite region of where we were! Maybe the ash we walked into was some sort of…

portal?"

"I'll take that explanation."

Makim observed his surroundings, "Sure, sure. Let's go with that. Huh. Well this place is much better anyways. It's not even that cold."

Naomi noticed the sound of running water nearby. She started running towards it, yearning for a drink to quench her thirst. Makim and Manny followed her and soon enough, they came across a crystal clear stream of chilled water. Naomi began drinking out of the stream as fast as she could, until she got a brain freeze and took a break. The gang filled up their canteens with the rich and chill stream water, and carried on.

It could've been days, or even weeks before they noticed any sign of life other than themselves. The region they were in proved to be quite massive, so massive in fact that they began to contemplate whether they were still even in Mai. All of their worries however, began to shift, when while they were eating frosted blueberries harvested from bushes they found nearby, they heard a rustling noise coming from some bushes a few yards behind them.

They all sprang around to see what was behind them. The sight they saw made Makim wish they were back in the Land of Embers. What laid behind them, hidden in the bushes, stood up. A 10 foot beast, seemingly made of body parts of a variety of animals that likely once roamed the lands.

It had eyes, but they looked dead. Its chest cavity was exposed and all the organs were in place, but they weren't pumping. It had all the organs you'd expect one to have. Except for a heart. But what was most disturbing about this creature to the gang, was that it looked as if it was created to be an exact replica of a tabby.

It spoke, "Naomi··· please, do me this one thing··· For my being to be complete··· Your heart, Naomi. It belongs to me."

"Uhh... no?"

"Please, my body can't live long without it. I need it. I NEED IT!!"

The creature lunged at the group but they were just fast enough to escape with their handfuls of blueberries and not stop until they found themselves running into a big open field. They took a moment to catch their breath, then tried to process what exactly they had seen.

"*huff*, guys... *huff*, what was that thing? Naomi, have you seen it before?"

"Oh yeah, I think it lives across from me- No, I've never seen that thing before Makim!"

"How'd it know your name?"

"I don't know!"

"Uhh I could care less about how it knows your name. Why does it want your heart?!?"

"I don't know!! Guys, stop asking me questions like I know the answers!"

"Let's just keep moving guys. Maybe there's a town or city somewhere nearby. Besides, I'm starting to get hungry."

Wandering through the forest was no longer an enjoyable experience for the gang. The slightest surge of wind led them to jump. The rustling of leaves sounded more like running. Paranoia was thick in the air. To that thing, however, this was simply a game of predator versus prey.

HERMAN 105 HARRISON

Composed of animal body parts. Was it created by

someone? Well, I'm not sure. But to Naomi that didn't matter.

She didn't want to think of it. All she wanted to do was get out

of the forest. Her wishes would only partially be met. Makim

eventually spotted an intimidatingly tall castle tower in the

middle of a frozen lake.

"Hey guys, look this way! There's some sort of castle

over here. Maybe there's someone there, or food."

As the gang got closer, the tower's true size began to

show more and more. It went so high you'd have to squint to

see the top. Looking up at it made Naomi dizzy. Naomi found

the main entrance, which was busted open. Big chunks of the

door were laying on the ground. It seemed someone had tried

to break in. Or out?

The team entered the castle, and upon entering, the

first thing they noticed was how the sunlight illuminated the

tower. It seemed there wasn't a closed roof. But the sunlight

was quickly fading, so they hurried up the excruciatingly long

staircase to reach the top.

"Maybe we'll find something useful here, to help me find

where I'm supposed to find my next element, ya know?"

"I guess so. I'm just hoping we don't run into that...

thing, again."

"Same here, Makim."

After not long, there was suddenly a thin layering of snow on the steps, and it gave a crunch to every step the team took up the stairs. The farther they got from the ground, the more apparent it was to them just how cold it was in the castle. Walking up twenty steps seemed to take half an hour out of the sunlight.

After further observation, Manny realized the stairs were made of selenite marble, a rare find, given its association with elementals of Tamiba City. All this walking gave the team some time for reflection.

Manny, grunting up the stairs, started reflecting outwards, "So... hey, Makim, what was life like living in Tamiba City before Solituno came?"

"Good question. To be honest, now that I think of it, It was pretty boring. At least before I met you. Day by day, nine to five, ya know? I'd get up, go to work, go back home, and sleep."

"Seems like a pretty nice lifestyle!"

Makim stopped for a moment, halting Manny and Naomi,

"If I'm being honest with you, it wasn't. It was

monotonous. But now, I feel like I'm doing something

important, ya know? Something bigger than me. So

yeah, that's pretty cool. I'm glad I got to meet you, both

of you."

"Same, Makim."

"I feel the same way guys! Hey... Manny, I just noticed

something! I have elemental powers, Makim has a sword...

What do you have to battle?"

"...The power of coersion?"

"Yep. That sounds about right. Cause that's gonna stop

whatever's gonna try to eat you alive. Oh! And maybe

they'll apologize too, and realize the errors of their

ways!"

"Alright, so maybe we need to get that sorted out."

Naomi chuckled, and Makim and Manny followed

soon after, "Enough of this chit chat guys, we came here

for the loot!"

"Makim, we're not 'looting', we're investigating!"

The team continued up the stairs. And you know what? Seemingly out of nowhere, it seemed to warm up just a small bit in the castle.

Soon enough, they made it to the top. The view was unsurprisingly marvelous. The sky was turning dark, but the top was illuminated by three large crystals, emitting a warm and bright yellow light. All three of them were floating, arranged in the shape of a triangle. Strane engravings were made on them that looked almost like drawings.

Other than the crystals, there was a small table with a chair, both made of mahogany wood, polished and painted light purple. The team was astounded by the sight. Naomi looked hard into the carvings on the crystals.

"Hey, Manny! This one right here kind of looks like a duck. You think maybe the person who carved this out is a duck or something?"

Manny objected, "Naomi, that's not a duck, that's

clearly a rabbit. I'm not sure what the meaning is behind it though."

"Whatever you say, pal. Wait a minute... are those scales? Do rabbits have scales?"

"Hey… you're right. Whatever this is, I've never seen anything like it before. Matter of fact, it's starting to give me the heeby-jeebies."

"Yeah, those eyes look dead-"

Naomi recalled the strange creature they saw in the woods earlier. Was the engraving on the crystal the same thing? "Multiple animal parts... Dead eyes... Manny, do you think this could be that thing that was chasing us earlier?"

"It could be! Now that I think of it, I'm pretty sure it had scales on its body, just like this nasty piece of art."

"So whoever carved this probably has something to do with why that thing exists."

"Yeah, most likely. No, definitely."

While Naomi and Manny tried to configure the meaning of the engravings on the crystals, Makim went up to the desk. Not so much looking for a way of direction, he sat on the chair, testing it's comfortability. Still, he looked at the plentiful items on the table.

There were matches, stitches, surgical knives…? Oh, and a diary of some sort. Makim decided to look into it with no hesitation. He skimmed for a while, then flipped quicker and quicker, then stopped, feeling he had gone far enough into the book.

"'January 13th. I am pleased to write today that Solituno Tali has finally been brought back to life. Eager is an understatement for how much I long to see the giant beast, for my own eyes.' What type of weirdo would root for Solituno? Don't they know it wants to destroy them just as much as everyone else?"

As irritating as it was for Makim, he kept reading the log, hoping he'd find some sort of twist where the writer changes their views.

"'May 21st. It seems as if though there may be a way to bring Solituno back, after it's astoundingly humiliating defeat' blah blah… 'by combining the bodies of the forest into one united being I will bring Solituno back once more through the very one that sent it back to whence it came...' Well, this sure was a find!"

Makim rushed to Naomi and Manny, now looking at another strange depiction carved onto another crystal.

"Guys, I think whoever's been hanging out at this castle created that thing that was chasing us earlier! More importantly, they've been fanning over Solituno, and want to bring him back!"

"Sounds about right. Well, is there any clue to where they are? So we can, well, deal with them?"

"Nope. Just pure weirdome. I say we get out of here. Maybe there's another castle, or a town, a place with people that can help us. Cause with all this new fallen snow out here, I don't think it'll do us any good trying to trace footprints."

"Alright, but let's sleep here for tonight."

"No way! What if this little weirdo comes here in the middle of the night to see us sleeping in their little abode? What if they turn us into a mix mashed walking monster too?!?"

"You've got a point. But it's dark out now. So, tell me genius, where do we go now?"

"Outside. Chop chop, carry on.. Back outside, we go. Maybe we'll find a real comfy pile of snow nearby. "

Just as they were readying to go back downstairs, Naomi caught out of the corner of her eye a large figure in the dark, quickly pacing towards the castle.

"Guys, let's get out of here! QUICK! There's someone coming, we gotta go!"

Cautious and speedy as they could, the gang scaled the stairs, jumped out the bursted door and ran as fast as they could out right into the middle of the dark forest. They turned back to see that no one had followed them, and were relieved. Until they realized, that they had ran into the middle of the dark forest. Then they stopped and ran through their options.

"Guys, *pant* I'm starting to think staying in the castle to face whoever was coming might've been a safer idea. We would've had the high ground, after all."

"Well as long as that thing doesn't come after us I think

we'll be just fine."

At that very moment, a dreadful howl, as loud as a siren, was released into the forest by something nearby. Likely that thing. The gang thought so too, and made a run for it in the opposite direction of where they thought the sound was coming from. They ran not long until they decided to find a place to rest for the night.

They decided on picking a small patch of land that was clear of foliage. Easy to look around, easy to move around and they got the best of the moonlight. Makim heard water running nearby.

"Hey guys, I'm starting to get pretty thirsty. Hear that crisp cold water? I'm sure it's not far, I'll go bring some back too. Just hand me your canisters."

"Sure Makim. Thanks for the water."

Makim began trekking into the forest, nearly entirely depending on his ears to find the water. When he finally did, he cupped some in his hands, and took a large gulp, then started filling up the canisters.

Now, you see, It was quite difficult for Makim to see

what was right in front of him, so when he got up from his fill of water, he didn't quite see anything much, but one thing he did hear was the hot breath of whatever was behind him. He left no time to think, assuming it was the doppelganger.

He ran and ran as fast as he could, but the footsteps behind him never seemed to get farther. Eventually he made it to the cleared out patch where the camp was. He finally jumped around to see what was chasing him, fully immersed in the illumination of the moonlight, and to no surprise, but all the dismay, it was the doppelganger creature.

"I don't know what you are, or why you're following us around, but you're about to find out what happens to people who can't use their words!"

Makim drawed his golden sword out, but the creature took no change in pacing. Once it got close enough, Makim swiped the doppelganger with his sword using all his might. It sliced an arm off. The doppelganger then slapped Makim across the ground like he weighed nothing, and was ready to crush him with its weight, until Makim's friends came just in the knick of time.

Manny was throwing pebbles at the monster, "Hey, did you get me some water? I'm kind of thirsty now."

"Shut up Manny! Get over here and help me find a way to beat this thing! I tried my sword and cut its arm off but it's not backing down!"

"Well, maybe you're just bad at getting people to back down."

Manny threw a slightly bigger pebble, a little harder, and that got the doppelganger's full attention, and it started charging his way.

"Don't try to fight it! Just try to throw stuff at it from a distance!"

"Trust me, I'm not trying to go anywhere near this thing!"

Amidst all this chaos, a certain Naomi had only just begun hearing the commotion going on outside the camp tent. She wasn't surprised to see it was the doppelganger. They locked eyes.

"Naomi, turn yourself to me and I will spare your friend's life."

"Hm... Nope, I think not!"

The doppelganger grew angered and started charging

at Naomi. Naomi remembered her new elemental power she had, and wanted to test run them on the doppelganger.

"Aye! Come here you fat lump of meat!"

I guess the doppelganger got offended, because it started growling. It was running towards Naomi in a drunken manner, and boy, for its size, it was FAST. The point of view must've been eerie for sure. Well, at least for the average person, but Naomi was prepared.

She channeled her elemental energy into a large fireball, about half her size. The doppelganger had no hesitation, running at full speed now. Naomi spun around with the fireball in her hand to gain momentum, tossed the fireball into the air, and with all her might, she kicked the fireball right into the doppelganger's face.

It was sent flying across the field, tumbling into the snow covered dirt. Naomi's stance softened, and she checked the doppelganger to see if it was still moving. It laid there, lifeless in the field. Makim and Manny followed suit.

"Welp. Looks like you killed it. That was pretty cool, I have to admit!"

"Thanks Makim! Wait... what's that?"

The sun had been rising over the horizon for some time, and in the golden light of the sun, something started shimmering in the doppelganger's mouth. Naomi pulled it out. Another emblem! This one had a snowflake on it. Another transformation was happening. Naomi then started emitting a strong white light from her eyes and started floating. She knew the drill by now, and so did Makim and Manny. Soon she fell back to the ground, and the emblem was no longer there.

"Wait, so do you have snow powers, or ice powers?"

"Both?"

"Let me test it out. Stand back guys!"

Naomi decided to target Makim's water canister. Naomi started taking deep breaths, and with each breath her blood got cooler. Her body temperature decreased drastically. She raised her arms and started swinging them around in a coordinated pattern to gain momentum, then a cold frost shot out of her arms onto the canister. Makim skipped to the canister and opened it.

"Is it frozen?" asked Naomi.

"Yeah, this is frozen alright!"

It had been a number of days since Naomi had gained her new power. She wasn't quite sure how it would come in handy though.

"Hey, guys, you think I could use my ice power to freeze Solituno, eh?"

Makim chuckled, "well maybe, and you could freeze its hot breath!"

The gang continued traveling through the tundra landscape. The monotonous array of colors began to take a toll on them. The land seemed to never end, as though they were walking in an infinite loop.

Eventually, they came across a city. It was quite random in fact, being placed in such a desolate land. It reminded Naomi of Calidum City. They approached the city and - like in the forest - there was no soul nor trace of life within it. Something was clearly off, but, going against their senses, the gang went into the city.

Manny challenged their decision, "Guys, this seems like a

pretty bad idea. I mean, I don't see anything dangerous around here but look! There's no one here. Maybe that means we shouldn't be here either?"

"Well maybe they have a curfew. I mean, it's dark out Manny. Naomi, don't you agree?"

"Yeah. Besides, whatever this city's about, I'm sure it's more interesting than wandering the tundra."

    Along their stroll in the city, they saw massive apartment buildings, and an array of fast food restaurants built into the buildings. There was food in the buildings according to their advertised services, but no one was there to cook them. Manny spotted an owl all alone, sitting at a coffee bar, sticking out like a sore thumb in the lifeless environment. He approached the owl. Its eyes were as deep blue as the ocean itself, and always looked like they were on the brink of tearing up.

"Hey! Excuse me, does this city have a population? 'Cause my friends and I haven't seen a single person other than you."

"Ohoho! Well my friend, this city, Aqussio City, is full of people! Maybe you ought to look around a while more."

"Umm, well thanks? Have a good one…"

"More to you! Don't make assumptions, my friend! That never ends well… Oh, and by the way, my name is Azulio! Remember it!"

"My name's Manny. Trust me, I won't forget your name."

The gang continued their venture through the city. Out of sudden intuition, they all entered a building with a neon red sign of a bowl of noodles. Manny, and surprisingly, Naomi as well, grew wary of the food, not knowing its origin. Makim, however, had enough of gathering berries in the tundra forest. He jumped over the service counter and started chowing down on the precooked noodles.

When he got his fill, they were readying to leave, but just as Manny was about to open the doors to the restaurant, out of the blue, a large wave of water about knee height began flooding into the city from the sewer system. Surprisingly, it was crystal clear.

"Guys, what's happening?!?"

"I don't know Naomi! I have no idea."

They thought for a moment on how they would safely leave the city, but they didn't need to, because the water had drained back into the sewer system before they came up with a decision.

Careful to make sure the water wouldn't come back, they left the restaurant. And to their surprise, the streets were filled with all sorts of forest animal citizens. They all seemed to be dressed in old fashioned formal attire.

"GUYS WHAT'S GOING ON? There wasn't a single person here, and now they just... spawn in? Manny, you're smart. You got any idea?"

"Somebody has to be playing some sort of trick on us, because there's no way of explaining what just happened!"

"Don't worry guys! I'll go talk to Azulio to get some answers."

"Makim wait!"

Makim approached Azulio, "Ehem... Hey there, how's it going? If I recall correctly, there was absolutely NO ONE out here just two minutes ago! Is that correct?"

"And who might you be?"

"Makim. Now, please answer, what's going on here?"

The owl did not answer. It gave a dead stare to Makim, and then flew off onto the tallest building in the city's roof.

"Guys, the owl.. Azulio is definitely up to this! Something's not right, we need to leave this city!"

"You're getting real angsty all of a sudden. What's wrong? What did he say?"

"It's not what he said, It's the way he looked at me! Like he was tryna warn me of something!"

The gang traced their steps back in a rush, refusing to acknowledge the other citizens out of fear. When they traced their steps all the way back to where they entered Aqussio City, there was no exit. The entrance had disappeared!

"Guys, this is crazy. This has to be some sort of illusion!"

Naomi pulled stones from the building walls with her

elemental energy and attached them to her feet. She then
began kicking the buildings that were blocking the original
entrance, but to her dismay she didn't even make a dent on the
walls. She then tried punching the walls with fists of fire, but
all it did was leave marks on the walls.

"Guys, either these buildings are made of some sort of
indestructible material or there's some sorta woozy super
power stuff going on here! After all that, this building should
have a big fat hole through it!"

Out of the blue (like much of what had been
happening), speakers spread out across the city began
creaking, then the voice of Azulio began speaking.

**"Naomi, Naomi, Naomi... I've been watching you
and your little friends ever since you came to the
tundra..."**

"Hey, Azulio! Get down from that tower and let us out of
here! I don't know what type of game you're playing here,
but it's not fun!"

**"Oh Naomi... Just let me speak for a moment. I
know you're upset, just let me explain. You**

remember that beautiful beast you mercilessly killed in the tundra? That was my creation.”

Naomi broke into a cold sweat, *“He's talking like he's my friend... But that thing was trying to kill me! Something's wrong with him...”*

“I designed it to be as similar to you as possible, in hopes of recreating your elemental potential in another being. And so I gathered all the creatures of the forest for a... ‘costume party’, and, well, sacrificed their lives to create something with elemental potential. It did have the element of ice, though I didn't give that to it - for I possess the element of water.”

“So... What is it that you want with me?”

“Let me be clear. Naomi, I want your powers. Give them to me, and I'll let you and your friends leave.”

“One, I don't even know how to give them away! And two, even if I did, I'd never give them away, especially not to a lousy creep like you!”

"Very well, then. Good luck on saving your little land of Mai, because I won't be letting you out anytime soon."

The speaker intercom screeched for a moment, then shut down. In an instant, all of the people in the city near the gang turned their heads to them, and out of their eyes shot a deep blue light, identical to Azulio's eyes.

They simultaneously began walking towards the gang. They were like a sea of zombies. The gang all scrammed away from the citizens, ran into a weaponry store, locked the door, and pulled down the curtains.

Makim was fed up, "Alright, I've had enough of this owl guy! We gotta take him down!"

"Exactly! But we have to find a way up the building. That guy's not coming down!"

Manny noticed the weapons on the wall of the store, and grabbed a bow and quiver.

"We're just gonna have to get there fast, and this time all of us will be able to fight!"

As swift as a mouse and sneaky as a cat, they ventured into the streets of Aqussio City. They were careful to not be spotted by anyone, which was a challenging feat, considering the amount of people that were out searching for them. They weren't far from the building, they just had to go through the square plaza, which was filled to the brim with "people". Still, seeing no other option, they made a run for it and were spotted.

Waves of animals began walking towards them, but none ran. The gang got to the building door, and the door was locked. Naomi began desperately punching the wall with fists of fire, but like the rest of the city, there was no damage she could do. It seemed her powers weren't always going to get them out of a pinch. The wave grew closer and closer. "Guys, we gotta do something else!" Makim shouted. "Yeah, no duh! What do you think I'm doing right now?!"

Manny then got an idea. He aimed his bow and arrow at the keyhole of the door and shot it. He broke the door lock, and the gang swarmed into the building, followed right by the wave.

It seemed it was now only a battle of speed, which the gang was winning by a landslide. They scaled the stairs, as many as there were and got to the top of the building. Azulio was startled by how quick they were able to get to the top. With no warning, Manny shot his bow and arrow right for the eye of Azulio, who dodged it, then flew into the sky. "Aww, come on! Don't go flying somewhere else!"

Azulio then swooped back down to the roof as fast as a blur towards Makim, and Makim drew his sword out. The sword and the beak of Azulio clashed, with sparks flying everywhere. While Makim's sword was undamaged, the beak of Azulio was chipped. Azulio was furious.

"To take such foolish actions as to challenge me? How ignorant. I will teach you a lesson, one that you will never forget!"

Azulio decided to lay off the close combat, and decided to flood the city, all the way up to the roof tops, drowning all of the people below. The water didn't stop at the roof tops though, it kept rising, as if the entirety of Mai was being flooded! In a panic, Naomi froze the water the gang was swimming in, and formed a raft.

Azulio then drew a large ball of water into the sky, then let it drop, right over Naomi, but Naomi pulled out a large white fireball, hotter than any fireball she had formed before. It struck Azulio, who fell from the sky into the water. Then there was silence.

Makim broke the silence, "Soo... Naomi, is he dead?"

"Probably, that fireball was really strong-"

Naomi was interrupted by the sudden strong current of the waters, which sent them soaring. A vortex had been created in the water, with Azulio in the center of it. He was using the last of his energy to enter into his full elemental power. The ice raft began encircling the vortex, getting closer and closer.

"EVEN IF I AM NOT ABLE TO DEFEAT YOU, I WILL MAKE SURE YOU GO DOWN WITH ME, YOU FOOLISH DELINQUENTS!"

The raft got closer and closer to Azulio, and as it got closer, Naomi got an idea, "Manny, hand me one of your arrows."

"Uhh ok."

Naomi then froze the arrow, making it so cold it could freeze anything that touched its tip.

"Shoot Azulio in his eye!"

"Will do!"

Manny then shot the arrow, hitting Azulio in the bridge of his eyes, freezing them along with the rest of his face. Then, all of the water began draining into the sewers, and the gang laid down on the ground, astounded by the battle.

The buildings began to fade out, which freaked them out, bringing them back to their feet. Naomi quickly got up to make sure Azulio wasn't still alive, and noticed his eyes were no longer present, but an emblem was laying in the eye of Azulio, with a water droplet marking. Naomi grabbed the emblem, and in an instant, she blacked out.

A familiar voice spoke, "NAOMI, NAOMI! OPEN YOUR EYES."

"Oritula! Wait, how are we talking? This hasn't happened with the other elements I've gotten."

"That's none of your concern. You have done so well Naomi. I must tell you though, Solituno is coming sooner than I had previously anticipated. I knew they were coming soon, but not this soon..."

"Uh oh."

"Do not worry, you now have the elemental powers of earth, fire, ice and water! It has been prophesied that you will possess earth, fire, ice, and water in the final battle. In addition to those, two more. One of them being momentum. "

"Ok, so one, that doesn't sound like a traditional element, and two, where and how do I find it?"

"Naomi, when you wake up, you will be in another place, along with your friends. They have fallen asleep along with you. I want you to know that everything in the tundra was an illusion, created by Azulio. When you took his element, you took control over his powers, and killed his illusion."

"What?!? Well, that would make sense. But where are we

going now?"

"I'M SORRY, I DON'T KNOW FOR SURE. THE ONE THING I CAN TELL YOU IS THAT YOU MUST MOVE URGENTLY! WHEREVER YOU LAND, MOMENTUM WILL BE YOUR NEXT ELEMENT TO MASTER."

"Alright Oritula. ...I'm starting to get worried. You saw how much I struggled to beat Azulio! If Solituno is supposed to be even bigger and stronger, in a whole new form, how am I gonna stand a chance against him?"

"NAOMI, FOR THE TIME BEING, YOU ARE BEING ACCOMPANIED BY YOUR FRIENDS. BUT I WILL BE DIRECT WITH YOU. WHEN THE FINAL BATTLE HAPPENS, NO ONE WILL BE ABLE TO HELP US. IT WILL ONLY BE ME AND YOU, AGAINST SOLITUNO."

"How is that supposed to assure me?!"

"WHAT I AM SAYING IS THAT YOU ARE DESTINED TO DEFEAT SOLITUNO. I CHOSE YOU AND YOU SPECIFICALLY FOR A REASON, NAOMI."

"What reason?!?" Naomi's voice broke. She began to tear up, "I've had to hurt so many people, I've had so many people want to hurt me. Why do I have to go through this, of all of the people in Mai you could've chosen?"

"Because you're the only one with a strong enough willpower to go through everything you've been through, because you know yourself, that you care enough to put aside your own feelings to save so many more people than you've hurt! Naomi, you will win. You need to keep your head up, and stay positive. That's how you beat Solituno the first time, after all."

Naomi wiped her tears, "I can try."

A brief moment of silence took place.

"...That's the best, and only thing you can truly do."

V

Momentum is Strength

I'm not even sure where to start… I don't even know how to explain how the gang got here, but when they all woke up, they were in yet another new place. Only this time, it was real. A large field of rock sculptures and stone hills, all bright neon and in an array of colors, as if the ground were made out of jawbreakers.

The sky was a dark pink, and the sun was stuck at a set. It almost looked like pink lemonade.

Makim freaked out, "ALRIGHT, WHERE ARE WE NOW?? I can't stand this! As far as I know we're not even in Mai anymore! Some other planet or something."

"Well Makim, Mai's pretty expansive, with vastly varying climates, so I wouldn't be surprised if we were still, well, in Mai."

"Guys, where are we?!? I need to find a way to master the element of Momentum!"

"Naomi, what are on about? What type of element would momentum be anyways?"

'I'm not sure, but we need to find it! I was speaking with Oritula Tali and I was told I need to master the element of momentum! They said I would find it! ...Where are we anyways...?"

Naomi looked around for a moment, then noticed a number of big brown blurs heading straight for them, at an alarmingly fast pace.

"Guys there's something coming towards us!"

Makim squinted at the blurs coming their way, "Hey guys, I think those are a bunch of roadrunners! I don't think they're gonna hurt us."

"And how exactly are you sure about that?!?"

"I know one from back in Tamiba City. It's hard for them to go at a normal pace, I'm sure if we just sit and wait they'll peacefully greet us."

And peacefully greet the gang, they did. Or, maybe not so peaceful, more so abruptly, but nonetheless no one was harmed.

The roadrunners halted right in front of Naomi, and the biggest roadrunner introduced themselves, "Ello matie, me name be Oscar, and who may yous be, aye?"

"Hey, my name's Naomi, and these are my friends Makim and Manny. You see, there's this guy called Solituno and we need to defeat them-"

"Solituno, aye? Oye, I ain't heard that name in quite some time. Reminds me of solitude. Whad'ya say fellas?"

"Oye oye, yea!"

"For sure, matie!"

"...Well, he's coming back, and I need help to find out where I'm gonna get the element of momentum so I can save all of Mai. There's no telling how much time I have left, this is really important!"

Oscar the roadrunner stood still for a moment, then started jumping up and down in excitement, "Oye, I know just what will help you! You see, me fellas and I, we're the ones of whom you are looking for! We control the element of momentum! Just us, yeh! No one else! And what I have here in my hand is a shiny emblem to give

to a deserving person!"

Oscar opened out his wings, to reveal a shiny emblem with

arrow lines engraved onto it. Naomi's eyes brightened, "That's

great! So, I can just take that, and we'll be one our way.."

Naomi reached out for the emblem, but Oscar closed his wing

and tilted his head up.

"Hah, you think I'd give this beauty away for nothing?

I'll tell you what. Answer me riddle, and you may have

the emblem you so desperately need... I can't run out,

since the world never stops moving, but for some

reason you think there not be enough of me! What

may I be?"

"You must not be getting this. I need that emblem to defeat

Solituno! If you don't give it to me, we'll all DIE!"

Manny stepped in, "Relax Naomi, I'm sure we still have t-"

"You don't get it! You don't know what I know! We have to

defeat Solituno, and to do that we need to get the element

of momentum! As soon as possible!"

Naomi, in a panic, lunged at Oscar, who then shook her off and jumped onto a pile of rainbow colored rocks.

"Oye, how rude of you! It be in your best interest to think about the riddle, because I won't be handing this emblem to yeh unless you answer it!"

Makim tried his hand at the riddle, "Is it... water?'

"Oye, no maytie!"

"Hm... basses?"

"Hah, of course not mate! My, you're a silly one."

"...Tuna croquettes?"

"Alright mate, that's enough guessing. I won't put a limit on how many tries you get, but don't be a bugger! Take time to think about the question, yeah?'

Seeing that Oscar would not be letting up the emblem without an answer to the riddle, Naomi stomped her way away from the rock pile, in hopes she would find a town, or city, and of course Makim and Manny tagged along.

"Hey sweetheart, maybe you should loosen up a bit and relax! You're acting like Solituno's coming right now."

"Yeah, Makim's right. Let's at least try finding out this riddle. You heard them! They're the last masters of momentum."

Naomi took a deep breath, then sighed, "Alright, fine. Let's try solving the dumb riddle."

The gang ventured, but not far from Oscar and his mates. They decided to go on a walk, to help Naomi calm her nerves down. They eventually came across a single wooden hut in the middle of an open field, covered with blue and red roses.

Intrigued by the hut, which stuck out from the fever dream-like environment they were in, they went to investigate. Naomi knocked on the door, and out of the door came a short, old teal dragon. Its scales were oval shaped and it had a monocle on. It had a yellow beard and mustache stretching down to its waist, and was covering its mouth.

"Hello there! The name's Naomi, and these are my friends Makim and Manny."

"Hello there, travelers! What brought you all the way here, to my humble home?"

"Well, this may seem a bit odd, but we were wondering if you could answer a riddle for us. We've been thinking about it for a while now and still can't think of an answer."

"Ooh, I sure do love riddles!"

The dragon's stomach grumbled, "Well… not on an empty stomach. Sorry, but I'm afraid there's no good I can do for you unless I have a meal."

"Ok then, go eat something! We can wait."

"Well, I would love to make a saimond milkshake. I have the milk and ice, but the only place I know of that has saimond berries is Moveil's Hill. It's not far from here, but my old bones certainly can't go there. I guess you'll have to find another person, travelers. Goodbye!"

"W-wait! We'll go get the saimond berries! Where are they?"

"Oh, you will? Why, how kind of you all! Well, just

follow the direction of the sun, and you'll come across the hill in no time."

"Sure thing! We'll get plenty for you."

"Thank you kind travelers, but I must warn you, there's been rumors spread by the forest creatures nearby that there's a dangerous beast lurking on the tip of the hill! So proceed with much caution! Good luck!"

"Thanks! We're fit for the job! Oh, by the way, I never got your name!"

"Ahh yes, my name is Moquteal."

"Wait a minute... so is Moquteal's Mt. in the Land of Embers named after you?"

"Hoho, why yes! I'm an old dragon, and I was the very first to climb to its peak! I made the trail that's now there. Matter of fact, Moveil's Hill is named after my older brother, Moveil. My family has a history of natural landmarks being named after them."

"Hey, that's pretty cool! Trust us, we're gonna get those

saimond berries in no time!"

So the gang set their direction for the sun, which was strangely set in the same place it was since they first woke up from their slumber. Looking to further appreciate the landscape, Manny noticed the abundant forest life in the forest surrounding the entire neon badlands field. Whatever foliage that was surviving in the neon badlands were either highly citrus fruits like lemons or limes or pink weeds.

Along the way to the hill, they came across a river which blocked the way to the hill. Not only that, but to pass the river by swimming was an obviously unwise decision, as this was no ordinary river. The liquid was purple, with large foam bubbles floating on top, and on top of that, the river was going at an alarmingly fast speed. On the positive side, the hill was within eye view.

"So, Manny, Naomi, how do we get across this river, huh?" Makim questioned.

Manny got an idea, "I suppose we could try swimming?" A bad idea is still an idea, but Naomi had a better idea. She started focusing on her breathing and took

deep breaths, and eventually her body temperature drastically

dropped. The average person's blood would be frozen or of a

slushy consistency, but not Naomi. She then blew over the

lake, freezing the water in an instant, leaving an icy pathway

across to the other side of the river. Even small waves from the

river's strong current were frozen in place.

 The gang crossed the lake with caution, and

continued heading on to Moveil's Hill.

"Nice going, Naomi."

"Thanks Makim. Let's hurry up and get to the top of the hill!"

 It wasn't long until the gang came across yet another

obstacle. There was a large ravine that seemed to stretch all

the way over the horizon. There was no way of walking

around. It was too long!

"Alright, how are we crossing this?"

Naomi already had an idea. She jumped up and struck the

ground with her fists, causing the ground to break into chunks.

"Ghaa! Naomi what on earth are you doing?!?"

"Just wait, you'll see!"

Naomi then morphed all of the rocks into a bridge. Naomi felt accomplished by her skillful use of her powers. As the gang was just about done crossing the bridge, three large bright red fireballs with cartoonishly angry faces came flying from the bottom of the ravine and landed right in front of them. They gnarled hard. For what reason they were mad, I'm not sure.

"Um... hello? Can you guys just move out of the way, and we'll be on our-"

"Us? Move? FOR WHAT?!?"

"...So we can pass. Look, we don't want any trouble, just let us cross."

"Well, I suppose we could let you pass just this one time. ARGH I can't believe I'm letting you go! Just this one time! If you come back, you're gonna get a face full of fiery fury in your face! RAAAA GO!"

The fireballs huffed and puffed. Naomi thanked them and the gang moved at a swift pace.

"Naomi, we're gonna have to cross again to get back to

Moquteal."

Unfortunately for the gang, the fireballs heard them, and were even more furious than before. They growled and jumped up and down, and their red color bursted into white.

"What's that I heard? You're still gonna come back, huh? I knew I should've taken you out right there and then! RAAAAH!"

One of the fireballs bounced themselves towards Makim, who sliced it in half with his sword. Now there were two smaller fireballs, who quickly grew back to their original size.

"Great going, I'm sure if you just keep slicing them up we'll get out of this!" Naomi said sarcastically.

"Aye, it's not my fault! I didn't know they could split!"

A fireball bolted towards Manny, who then shot an arrow at it. Of course, it went right through the fireball, and Manny started running.

"Hey! Fellas! Let's all attack that tabby! She's the one who built that ugly bridge on our beautiful ravine!"

All four of the fireballs bolted towards Naomi, as angry as can be, but Naomi channeled into her water powers and lifted a wall of water, and the fireballs had no choice but

to sit in their anger, and wait for her to come out.

"Wait, um... angry fireball guys, are you mad because of the

bridge I made?"

"Of course, you dumbhead! Why'd you make it so UGLY?!?"

"Well, what can I do to make it not so ugly?"

"How about BURNING IT!!"

"I can do that, just wait a minute!"

"Wha-? I was being sarcastic, you dummy!"

Naomi didn't hear the enraged fireball. She put down

the water wall, ran to the bridge, and went to work, blowing

fire on the stones that made the bridge. The fireballs watched,

too stunned to keep fighting. When Naomi had finished, the

stones were charred, making the bridge charcoal black.

"How about that? Are you happy now?"

"We.. ABSOLUTELY... LOVE IT!!!!" The fireballs started bouncing, now

from happiness instead of anger. Their color turned a deep

dark red. **"And, oh, sorry about causing a ruckus with you and your fellows. But**

you gotta admit, this bridge was UGLY before you charred it up! When you come

back we won't bother you. Carry on!"

"Yeaaaah, have a good day!"

It seemed combat wasn't the only way to quell an enemy. The gang kept moving, getting closer to the top of the hill, and as they got closer there was more and more foliage, blending in with the rock terrain. It seemed that everything was alive on the hill. The flowers smiled, the tulips chuckled and even the weeds mumbled.

It seemed like a fairy tale world, like they were living in the mind of a child. Makim wasn't too happy about how lively everything was, 'This place feels too happy... We're getting close to the top of the hill. Whatever horrible creature's up there, I'm not so sure I wanna face."

"Makim, you've got no choice! The ice path I made at the river's probably melted by now. Don't worry, Whatever's up here, I'm sure we'll be alright."

They soon reached the top, which had a large tree with marks all over it. Manny spotted a large figure around the tree. It had at least 40 long tentacles squirming around.

"Guys, there's some sort of monster around the tree! Get

prepared to fight!" Manny shouted to the enemy, "Show yourself!"

The creature slowly crept around the tree, to reveil their identity. What came around the tree was about 40 large pool noodles… attached to a small pale dragon.

"Huh? Who are you?" Manny asked.

"Why, I'm Moveil."

"…Ohhh! Heh, with those pool noodles on your back, the shadow I saw looked like some crazy monster!"

"Ohoho, no monsters here! Just this saimond tree."

"Saimond tree? Say, could we have some of those berries? We actually met your brother Moquteal earlier today, and he'd like to have some."

"Moquteal? Well, of course, take as many as you need! Ohoho, he's always loved these little tasty berries."

The saimond berries were ripe and green. They were like tiny limes, with specks of blue everywhere. Manny picked some of the berries and put them in a satchel.

"Thanks for the berries! Oh, and why do you have those pool noodles on your back, anyways?"

"Efficiency, my boy! Rather than carrying pool noodles to the river, I simply walk there with them on my back, so I can plop right into the river and float!"

"Clever… well, we'll be on our way. Have a good one!"

The gang got back to Moquteal's hut, and Manny handed him the berries.

"Hohoho! Thank you, travelers! Now I'll make us all a delicious saimond milkshake!"

The gang sat and waited while Moquteal prepared the smoothie, and soon Moquteal finished blending the saimond berries. He handed the milkshakes to the gang. Makim took a sip of the milkshake, and scrunched his face.

"This is really… sour. But it's good!"

"Hey, thanks for the milkshakes. Will you answer the riddle now?"

"Ahh yes, my apologies Naomi. What was the riddle

that you wanted answered?"

"It went something like... I can't run out, since the world never stops moving, but for some reason you think there isn't enough of me. What may I be? Got any ideas?"

Moquteal stood frozen, thinking hard on the riddle.

"Well, traveler... This riddle... I can't seem to find an answer to it. I'm sorry. Oh! Just give me a moment to look in my library room, I might come back with an answer."

'And how long exactly is that gonna take?"

"Four years or so. I have a lot of books! You can stay here in the meantime."

Naomi sighed, "That's alright. This riddle needs to be solved before then. We'll just hang a little while longer then be on our way."

"I'm really sorry to put you through all of this trouble for no reason, travelers."

Manny chimed in, "Don't sweat it! This was pretty enjoyable compared to what we're used to."

"Well, I'll be going to my den now *yawn* travelers,

please lock the door when you leave. Have a good evening."

And so Naomi, Makim and Manny sat, sipping their milkshakes. Makim was gulping his milkshake up as if it was going to disappear. Naomi couldn't help but notice, "Makim, chill out, you're gonna end up getting a brain freeze! We've got time... time? ...TIME!" Naomi had made a revelation, "Guys, the answer to the riddle has to be time! It doesn't run out, and well... Now, I'm starting to think I have time. Maybe I've got a chance at beating Solituno. But I thought I didn't have enough of it!"

Makim chimed in, "Huh.. That makes sense! And hey, Naomi, I'm glad you've chilled out. I guess it's because of this little quest's change in pace. ...Looks like we've all finished our milkshakes, heh. So I guess it's time to go, yeah?"

"Yeah."

Oscar was still perched on the glowing neon rock

pillar he had been on since the gang left. He spotted the gang

and jumped way high in the sky, flapping his wings to break

his fall. Naomi approached the bird, "Alright Oscar, I'm ready."

"Right then, here we go again! ...I can't run out, since

the world never stops moving, but for some reason

you think there not be enough of me! What may I

be?"

Naomi took a moment, then smirked, "Time."

"Oye, oye! Congratulations my friend, you answered

the question correctly this time!"

"Heh, thanks! Only you've got one thing wrong."

"Hmmmm?? And what might that be?"

"I don't think there might be enough time anymore. Now, I

KNOW there's ENOUGH time."

"Well then, even if you didn't, I think you'll have no

problem having it with this."

Oscar opened up his wing and handed Naomi the

emblem. Naomi reached out and grabbed the emblem. She

began floating and her eyes began to glow a bright white light.

Eventually the light faded back into her, and she fell back on her feet. The emblem was no longer in her hand.

"Naomi mate, you now have the power of momentum!"

"...What exactly is that? Hehe... I kinda forgot to ask earlier."

"Who in the land on Mai would not know what the power of momentum is? *sigh*, Well, momentum isn't exactly a traditional element, I guess. It's more of a boost of the skills you already have. With momentum, You'll be able to move waaay faster than you've ever gone before! I mean cheetah fast!"

"Cool! That sounds like it'd be pretty handy-"

"I'm not finished either mate! On top of that, your strength will be increased and you'll be able to jump super duper high! But do be careful, friend! If you get too caught up in the motions, you may end up losing control of where you're going!"

Naomi grinned, then jumped up, and kicked the

ground hard, lifting herself yards up into the air, effortlessly. She ran all the way to Moquteal's hut and back within minutes, no sweat. She could feel she was much stronger than before. She felt sure she could face any enemies that might come her way.

"Hey guys, what's next?"

"Naomi, I think the better question would be WHERE EVEN ARE WE? I've never seen a place like this in Mai ever before!"

"Right, Makim."

Oscar spoke up, "Oye good ole mate, you've been a delight, why don't you have this map? We're right in the bottom left, you see."

Naomi examined the map, "Hey… guys, we're right next to my hometown! If we just go through the marsh forest hugging up on this badland field, we'll be there in no time!"

"Naomi, that's awesome! Hey, are we gonna meet any old friends you got, huh?"

"Well yeah Makim, I've got a good friend, Wisely back there.

I can't wait to see the look on his face when he sees all of
what I can do now!"

And so, our three heroes had made way for the
marshy forest, and it seemed that Naomi had gained back her
eagerness for adventure! She walked with a skip, smiling and
humming. Whatever form Solituno was coming back in,
Naomi was sure she could handle it. It didn't hurt that Makim
and Manny believed she had it in her as well. I'm sure we all
believe she has what it takes.

VI

Only Time Will Tell

The marsh forest was no joke. Purple vines wrapped around carsh trees, which were large hollow trees that grew in wet environments. When the dry season takes place before winter hits, the ground is still hazardously slippery, and the trunks of the trees expand.

When winter hits, the trunks curl upwards to form root pillars, and when summer comes, the roots fall back down in the water, and the trunks shrink back up. Traversing the forest would've been hard enough, because of the high waters that could at times reach up to a person's neck, but thankfully it was just about dry season, so the water only reached Naomi's ankles.

The trees had an oddly pleasing scent to them, something like potent lavender, giving the forest a sweet scent. Slish sloshing about the forest wasn't all bad, though, mostly because of the sweet lupina berries that grew from the base of the carsh trees. The gang ate plenty, which gave them energy to keep moving.

The lack of wildlife made the marsh forest dead

silent, other than the occasional wind drift and sloshing of the gang's feet. The silence drew Makim crazy, and he began to speak, "So Manny, how's it going with that bow, huh?"

"Pretty good Makim. Well, fine actually. I just wish I got to use it more."

"What do you mean? You can still use it!"

"Yeah, but… We all know the final battle between Naomi and Solituno's coming pretty soon. I mean, Naomi's gonna win of course, so we don't have to worry. But after that, what would we have to do after that? There wouldn't be any enemy to fight."

"Well, just remember how we started this journey. We didn't start it for a reason, the reason came to us. We still haven't gone everywhere in Mai, so there's probably a whole other world of crazy stuff we could get into!"

"I get what you're saying Makim."

Eventually the gang found a way out of the marsh forest, which opened up onto the Seaside Park. They were back in Naomi's hometown.

"So this is your town, huh? Pretty nifty!"

"Thanks Makim. It feels like it's been so long since I've been here! Man... Guys, let's go to my house!"

"Lead the way!"

The gang made their way to Naomi's home, and along the way Manny realized just how vacant the town was.

"Seems like there's not many people here, huh? Did something happen?"

"No, it's always been this way. Most people that are still here are elderly. It's peaceful, quiet... But so boring!"

The gang got to Naomi's home, and Naomi got out her keys, and opened the door. When she went in, it was just as she left it - cluttered.

"Huh, you sure do have a lot of stuff here. How do you keep track of it all?"

"Hehe, well I've got my own system going on right now, I just find things when I need them! I'm kind of hungry, so maybe I'll look for something to eat. You want anything?

"Yeah sure. You got any... protein bars?"

Naomi reached her arm into one of the piles of cluttered items and pulled out a protein bar. "You see? I can just find stuff! Oh, guys! Let's go to where my friend Wisely's at!"

The gang made way for Wisely. When they arrived, Wisely set his eyes on Naomi, and his eyes widened like never before.

"Naomi! I knew we would meet again!" Wisely laid his eyes on Makim and Manny, "And who might these friends be?"

"Hey, the name's Makim. It's nice to meet you!"

"And my name's Manny. Same as Makim, It's nice to meet you!"

"My, oh my, what unique tales have you two gone on with Naomi? Tell me!"

Makim started running off on their adventures, "Well, for me personally, I met Naomi in Tamiba City. I'm part of a music group with Manny, she auditioned and got the job, and well, then Solituno came and-"

Wisely's eyes gaped, "Solituno? The spirit of vengeance, hatred, jealousy and misery?"

"Oh, don't worry though, it's been defeated!"

"By whom? I must meet with them!"

Naomi waved her hand up, "Wisely, it was me! Solituno came out and had everybody in Tamiba city under this sort of mind control, then they tried to eat me! But I kind of lit up in the sky, and woke up in some white void with Oritula-"

"Oritula Tali?? The spirit of joy, love, determination and hope?!?"

"Yeah! Anyways, after that I popped Soliuno from the inside out and they shattered into a bunch of pieces. I'm surprised You haven't heard about this Wisely."

"Naomi, you know I'm not one to watch television. My oh my. Naomi, you have grown so much since we last saw each other."

"And that's not all!"

Naomi then ran a few feet from Wisely, and stomped on the ground. The ground grumbled, and clumps of rock flew into the air. Then Naomi jumped way into the sky, even higher than the peak of Wisely's branches.

She began juggling balls of ice, fire and water. If Wisely weren't a tree, he would've needed to sit down. Naomi dropped the elemental spheres, then made a delicate landing back on the ground.

"What'd you think of that, eh?"

"I loved it! Wow… Naomi, I wasn't quite aware of your elemental potential! You are a tabby, after all. But how'd you achieve these forms so quickly?"

"Heh, well I sure did push the limit, plus, with the help of Oritula it's been a breeze figuring out how to use these powers!" Naomi's smile straightened out, "But Wisely, the battle's not over. Oritula told me Solituno's gonna come back again, SOON."

"My oh my… Naomi, I have something important to tell you." Naomi plopped herself on one of Wisely's roots, and so did Makim and Manny. "There is another prophecy that I know of, that there will be another coming of Solituno, where they will reach strengths no mortal alone can face. Solituno would face the one that would be called the greatest hero of Mai, connected with Oritula, so that they may channel into their full elemental power. Naomi, I believe you will be the greatest hero of Mai, and defeat Solituno once for all."

"Well that sounds like good news to me!"

"Yes, indeed. But given neither Solituno nor Oritula can be destroyed forever, I'm not sure what you will have to do to defeat Solituno. The prophecy almost seems contradictory… But I can give you one thing that may help you in Mai's deciding hours."

"What is it?"

"Naomi, I hold the elemental power of fusion."

"Another element, huh? What does it do?"

"Even I don't know, but It was passed down to me by a great elemental deity millenia ago, the same one who told me the prophecy of the greatest hero of Mai."

"Well, I guess it won't hurt if I get one more element…"

"Good, now rest both your palms on me."

Naomi then rested her palms on Wisely's trunk, and a glowing lime green light spurred out of where her hands were placed. Naomi didn't float this time, nor did her eyes glow.

"So... Do I have the element of fusion now?"

"I believe so, Naomi."

"How am I supposed to know how or like, when to use it?!?"

"...Only time will tell."

VII

When All's Said and Done

HERMAN 166 HARRISON

It had been a number of days since the gang arrived

in Naomi's hometown. Makim and Manny slept at Naomi's in

the night. They would play video games and play songs. For a

moment, life almost seemed normal.

Still, the lingering unavoidable fate that was the final

coming of Solituno laid over their heads, but Naomi was

peaking in confidence. She had powers few had, after all.

Makim had brought Naomi's TV down to Wisely so they

could all watch TV. Wisely grew fond of the TV, being

exposed to the current world of Mai through the television

screen, a spectacle he'd never seen before.

A particular evening had come across, when the sky

was unnaturally dark and cloudy, opposing the typically warm

colored sky. It was strange. The winds began to pick up a

little, just enough to lift fallen leaves from Wisely off the

ground. Manny turned on the TV to pick up on the latest

events going on in Tamiba City.

He turned the screen on to find that the weather was

drastically worse than the weather they were experiencing.

The sky was practically as night, even though it would've

been noon for the city, and the winds were beginning to uproot

trees in the city park. The much praised Tamiba City weather

reporter, J Pelird, spoke on the unusually aggressive weather.

"...and for all of those of whom that reside in the Land of Mai, I do

highly recommend you seek shelter in a bunker or evacuate

IMMEDIATELY. Radar scans detected unnaturally high wind speeds

coming in, and you can see the effects that these winds have had on

our beautiful city park. The current situation will certainly not be

getting any better, with even stronger winds being predicted and

thunderstorms coming in strong from the north. Stay safe out there,

citizens of Tamiba City, and stay safe, people of the Land of Mai. We

will now roll to street footage of the natural mayhem taking place

here. J Pelird, signing off."

"Hey, guys, get a look at this! Some crazy weather's

showing up in Tamiba City!"

Makim dipped his head down to the television screen, "Huh.

Maybe that has to do with the weather that's popping

up over here. What type of crazy weather is this? So

sudden..."

"...I have a feeling we're going to be given an answer to the strange phenomenon happening around the Land of Mai, sooner than later."

"I get what you're putting down... But I don't know if we're all the way ready yet. Well - not US, but Naomi. We still don't know what her fusion powers do, and she doesn't even know for sure if she has them! She can't use them!"

Naomi chimed in, "Well thank you very much Makim for the worries, but I'll be fine. I don't think you realize how much I've grown man, I can do this!

"Well, I'm not doubting your abilities, I know you're awesome and all. I'm just saying, fusion doesn't seem like something we can rely on."

"Who said we'd need fusion? I have other powers, Makim."

Manny chimed in, "Let's not forget Solituno's pattern of taking a different form every time they come back. Heh, what if they come back as a bug?"

"Then I'll squish them into a pancake."

The live footage on the TV began to break out, then

when it cleared, a gargantuan vein had opened in the sky, with

sickeningly thick dark purple smog falling out of it. It was

raining poison. Wisely's face creaked. By now there was no

one in the city; they all evacuated far from Tamiba City.

It seemed everyone watching the live footage in Mai

knew what to expect coming out of the vein; Solituno. But no

matter what they expected, they surely couldn't have expected

Solituno to come out in the freakish form they made for

themselves.

Out of the vein a dragon head peeked, just like

Solituno's, only tenfold larger. Then another dragon head

squeezed out, and then the head of a lion. They were all

connected to the same body.

"Alright, how many guys are coming out of that vein?!?

Guys, I don't remember Solituno having a twin."

"Naomi, Solituno definitely did NOT have a twin..."

The necks of the creature's heads were long and

thick, like the body of a snake. They all squirmed through the vein. When it was time for the torso to come out, there was a great struggle.

Even with the giant vein open, there wasn't enough room for Solituno to fit through. So then, Solituno tore the vein further open and their full body came through. 12 pairs of thick legs, some as big as a building, others as small as a door. Some legs had hooves, others with talons. The base of the body was still a dragon, with sharp scales angled just right for reaching wind cutting speeds.

Solituno's wings kept them afloat in the sky, with each flap causing gusts of wind that could be felt from blocks away. The front pair of wings were covered in obsidian scales, while the back wings were covered in long pearly white feathers. Solituno came to a rest on the tallest building in Tamiba City, causing the building to crack. It's tail wasn't so much of a tail, more of a large mass of tentacles attached to it's back. It seemed that being in such a rush to come back into the physical world led to their physical form being a much more abominable sight.

"Sooo... Naomi. You sure you wanna take this guy- or, thing, down?" Makim asked.

"Yeah, of course I want to defeat Solituno! Hurry, let's get going!"

"I won't lie Naomi, I'm staying as far back from that thing as I can. It's horrifying! I don't want to see it in real life."

Wisely said his final remarks, "Naomi, I believe it's time. Though this foe may seem to be giant, and gruesome, you WILL win. No matter how big and threatening Solituno attempts to become, you can always break through them!"

"Thanks Wisely. Rest assured, because I will defeat Solituno once and for all! Alright guys, let's get going!"

It took five days for the gang to arrive at Tamiba City in Naomi's stone suit, just like the one she made in the desert region. Along the way they had picked up a variety of clothes from other towns and cities, as gifts from shopkeepers who wanted to thank Naomi for her service. A pair of fire resistant boots from the Land of Embers… a sand cloak from Calidum City… and a pair of neon orange pants from the neon badlands (straight from Moquteal's personal collection).

Naomi knew she wasn't just given the clothes to look cool. She knew each piece of clothing represented a part of Mai she was fighting to keep safe from Solituno. When they arrived at Tamiba City, the sky suddenly darkened. Naomi hopped out along with Makim and Manny and made their way to Solituno.

Something about the air felt off - it gave Makim a subtle wave of anxiety, added on to the weight of having to bring Naomi to face Solituno.

"Guys, is it just me, or, is this place giving you a bad feeling?"

"Yeah, no duh you've got a bad feeling. Naomi's gonna battle the literal embodiment of evil. And it's gonna be many times stronger!"

"Ok, just checking..."

Just as expected, Solituno was atop the highest building in Tamiba City, and wasn't hard to find. Its wings casted a shadow over the entire block it occupied. Naomi knew Solituno was much bigger, but seeing the true magnitude of Solituno in person, was something hard for her to entirely process. They crept their way into the building and began the trek to the top.

"Hey Naomi, have you thought of how exactly you'll be defeating Solituno?"

"...Good point Makim."

"YOU DON'T KNOW HOW YOU'LL BEAT SOLITUNO?"

"Relax Makim! Hm... I guess... Oh! Last time, I was in Solituno's body and I... I had my drums, and I bursted Solituno from the inside out."

"Well you don't have your drumset now. So, what's the plan?"

"..."

"...?"

"...! Alright, so here's the plan. When I get up there, I'll get Solituno's attention, then If it tries to hit me or something I'll grab onto them and run onto their back. No way Solituno can reach their back, right? Then, I'll hit them with every last bit of every elemental power I have, right on their back!"

"Seems like a decent plan. You're really gonna have to give it your all Naomi. 'Cause from seeing the size of Solituno, I'm surprised this building hasn't collapsed. Even without force, their weight is dangerous."

"Well, then maybe Solituno should change their diet."

The team chuckled, embracing the moment. Everything was pointing in the direction of victory. It seemed Solituno hadn't yet seen Naomi, though it was expecting her.

They had reached the final floor, right below where Solituno was. The room was dark, with the only light illuminating it being the weak light from outside. Makim and Manny knew that they couldn't come with Naomi, for they might've been destroyed.

"Hey, kid... I just wanna let you know, I know I pick at you a lot, but I'm proud of how far you've come. Look. When this is all over and done, maybe I could teach you how to use a sword, eh?"

"Wow... thanks Makim, that's not like you! I'd love to learn from you."

Manny chimed in, "I think she'd rather learn to use a bow, heh."

"I can learn both guys!"

"Alright Naomi, go out there and save the day. Again."

"I will."

THE FINAL BATTLE

Naomi walked up the last steps, to stand on the rooftop of the building, and witness Solituno in all its capacity. Any normal person would freak out, but not Naomi. No, she stood firm, bold as a rock.

Then, she called out to Solituno, "Aye, look at me, you big fat freak!"

All three of Solituno's heads dipped down to Naomi, "I knew you'd come for me."

"I'm here to take you down... again! No, for the final time!"

Solituno began chuckling. Then laughing, laughing hysterically. Then they abruptly stopped, straight faced.

"I must admit, you had me stunned the first time, Naomi. But I'm not the same foe you once faced. Heh, go ahead. I'll let you take the first blow."

Naomi was stunned by Solituno's offer, *"What's up with Solituno? This isn't some game,... I gotta do something though!"*

Naomi pounced up into the sky and landed on Solituno's lion head. She blew a strong force of wind, as cold as ice. Solituno shook their head and Naomi fell off. She then pulled a large clump of stone from the building up to her using her earth powers, and while falling, she kicked the stone straight at the lion head.

Solituno was not affected. Solituno smirked, **"You haven't gotten much stronger. Maybe..."** Solituno raised their lion head way up into the sky, **"Just maybe,.."** Solituno whipped their head down to Naomi, **"You should've thought twice..."** Solituno slammed Naomi down into the roof of the building, **"Before coming to fight ME."**

Naomi was slammed all the way down to the ground floor of the building. She laid there, hazed and staring into the sky, unable to move, and fell unconscious. It seemed that Naomi had lost the battle.

Naomi woke up in a dark room. Oddly enough, she didn't feel any pain from being slammed through the building. She couldn't see anything, and started stumbling through the room to find a light switch. She scanned the walls with her hands, but before she could find the lightswitch herself, a door opened with a figure coming in, and they turned on the lightswitch.

The room, now illuminated, was revealed to be brown, and covered in illustrations. Naomi looked at the person who turned the light on, and it was Makim.

"Hey, you're up! ...How're you doing?"

"Where...? Where am I? What happened?"

"Heh, that's a long story. I'll tell you later. How are you?"

"I'm... feeling good! But, how? You saw what happened, right?"

"Yeah, I saw you fly straight through the roof and into the ground."

Naomi began smirking.

"What - are you laughing?!? How is that funny?"

"Wait no! It's not funny, it's just, imagining it in my head..."

"Maybe you aren't all the way back... come with me. You wanna know how you got healed? I'll show you the people who saved you."

Naomi followed Makim outside the room into the outside world.

"A town? We haven't been here before." Naomi wanted answers, **"Hey Makim, where are we?"**

"In the village of Mai."

The village was small, but full of tabbies. Makim eventually put Naomi to a stop, to a hut. In the hut, there was Manny, and a dark gray tabby, sipping on tea.

"Hey, Mafilius, this is Naomi."

Mafilius, the tabby, got up and approached Naomi.

"Ahh, I see you're finally awake. Hello Naomi. I am Mafilius."

"So, you helped me? How?"

"I hold the element of healing. I can heal the most injured of peoples."

"Wow... Thank you, I'm grateful for your help. But still, how'd we all get here? Is Solituno still in Tamiba City?"

"That's a long story, my friend. So, let me start from the beginning..."

PAST: TAMIBA CITY

Makim and Manny ran down to the bottom floor, to see Naomi's almost lifeless body laying on the floor, bruised, and with large gashes along her body.

Makim tried calling out to her, "Naomi? Naomi! Naomi, can you hear me?"

"Makim, she's unconscious! We need to get her out of here! Fast!"

Makim, in a panic, tried to lift Naomi up. Manny helped, and they ran out of the building in a hurry.

"Manny, we gotta get outa here! Fast!"

"Fast won't do. We don't have her stone suit! We'll just have to be stealthy."

They got in no more than a couple steps before

Solituno called out to Makim and Manny, **"FOOLS."**

They froze still, hoping somehow, someway, Solituno wasn't talking to them.

"Do you not hear me? Face me at once! Your little tabby hero is no longer. If you don't follow my orders, I WILL destroy you!"

They didn't listen, instead they ran as fast as they could, out of the city. Solituno was ticked off, and tried to swoop down to them to smash them with body weight alone, but Solituno was so big that the buildings blocked Solituno from reaching the ground.

Eventually, Makim and Manny made their way to a river system along the outskirts of Tamiba City, but Solituno had not left them alone. Solituno then swooped its feathered wing across the gang, but Makim had pulled his sword out at the last moment, keeping them safe, though they were still sent flying into the air.

"Manny! What are we gonna do now?"

"Land in the river!"

And so, they landed in the river, and after no time, the river opened out into the ocean. Makim was holding

Naomi, and was gasping for air, struggling to stay afloat, and Manny swam over to help him.

From a distance they saw a small boat coming their way, and they held out as long as they could, then the sailor on the boat called out to them, "Hop on! Quick!"

They wasted no time and got on the small boat, just in time in fact, because Solituno had catched up to them and slammed its tentacle tails into the water, creating a mighty wave. Instead of the boat being destroyed, it was sent soaring into the ocean. Makim spoke to the sailor, "Thank you for saving us. If I may ask, who are you?"

"My name is Mafilius, and I come from the village of Mai."

Manny inquired, "VIllage of Mai? I don't remember seeing that on any map."

"It's on an island, way off from here. I can take you there if you need. I can help your unconscious friend over there."

"We would be very grateful, thank you."

"It will take time though, we're far from the coast of Mai."

"Lead the way. Anywhere's better than here"

PRESENT: VILLAGE OF MAI

"...And that's how you got here, Naomi. Solituno's spread its influence along the majority of Mai by now."

"Hmm... Thank you all for helping me get better. Without you, I'd be done for. I guess my elemental powers weren't quite enough to beat Solituno... And they're only gonna get closer and closer to here... I'm sorry I couldn't save you all."

"Wait, you have elemental powers?"

"Yeah, fire, earth, ice, water, uhhh momentum and.... fusion?"

"Did you say… fusion?"

"Yeah. Why, what's up?"

Mafilius ran out the room in a hurry, and soon came back with a village elder, who then spoke to Naomi.

"Hello, all. I am Mapondius, descendant of Mai, the hero of, well... Mai. Naomi... greatest hero of Mai... The prophecies must be true then, yes yes..."

Naomi sighed, "What prophecy is this now?"

"The element of fusion was said to be a powerful one, Naomi."

"Oh yeah? Well if it's so powerful why can't I use it? It's dumb!"

"Oh it's not dumb, Naomi. You just haven't tried channeling it in another way than using it to attack."

"...Huh? What are you talking about? What else would it be used for?"

"Naomi, elements can damage, and elements can mend. You choose to use your powers to damage, much like Solituno."

"Hey, that's not true! For your information I can make a nifty stone suit, thank you very much!"

"Naomi, listen. Some elements are made out to cause destruction, and some made for people to form new entities with them. Fusion is neither, a bridge between the two. A connection between one another."

"And how exactly will this help me to defeat Solituno?"

"Naomi, Solituno was never created, and can never be destroyed. But they can be put in a form in which they can no longer cause harm to the world, and that's by using fusion."

"Ok, and...?"

"....well, hehe, the records don't say much on HOW to

use fusion, but they give little hints, or so it seems…"

Mapondius then opened a scroll book laying in the corner of the room, then slipped through the papers, "The text seems to be incoherent, but I know it has something to do with fusion… Ahh yes, here it is. 'A fusion touch is one that finishes… one that ends, and never replenishes… a fusion touch, oh what I'd do to have it… to become one with those of whom I once claimed to be my foe… for what I've tried so hard to defeat… has turned me a monster, and has left me weak…' really weird, huh? I'm not sure how to interpret this, but It seems it has to do with a 'fusion touch'."

"Fusion touch? Huh? Like if I–"

Suddenly the ground began to shake. Everyone struggled to stay standing, and books fell off the shelves they were kept on. They all ran out to see that Solituno had reached the island, and landed on the shore.

"Uh oh. Naomi, if you have any last chance of saving whatever's left of Mai, you're gonna have to find a way to use fusion touch."

"I think we're doomed then."

"WHAT?"

"Guys, I can't figure out how to use it! I've barely had any time to try!"

Solituno then began swiping the islanders up into the sky, and swallowing them whole, and Solituno began smashing the homes in the village with their wings. There was nowhere left to run, nowhere left to hide.

Naomi began walking towards Solituno, seeing that there was nowhere left to go. She didn't know if she could beat Solituno. Matter of fact, she wasn't planning on fighting Solituno. Something deep within her told her, *"This isn't how it has to end. Not for me, not for Makim, Manny, Wisely - No one!"* She didn't know what she was planning on doing, but she knew she had to make a move.

Naomi then ran, straight towards Solituno, and Solituno caught sight of her. In a sudden blitz of fury and rage, Naomi hurled a large formation of fire and rock, which turned into molten lava around her, and pounced on Solituno, who used their weight to charge into her, creating a large explosion, which blasted them both back, clouding the entire island. When it cleared, Naomi laid there, still as a rock. Unlike the last encounter, when Mafilius tried to heal her, she did not

come back. It seemed, that Naomi had finally died.

"Oh great. I'm here again. What now? Did I die or something?"

"Naomi, it is I once more, Oritula Tali."

"Alright, listen here! What's happening Oritula? What happened to my friends? Help, I need to get out of here and back to Mai!"

"Naomi, stop panicking! All this time, and you still don't seem to realize that you are DESTINED to win this battle."

"But... I'm dead, right? I'm done right? There's no going back. I failed."

"Naomi, You're forgetting that we both possess the physical body in which you reside. This battle is not over, no, most definitely not."

"So.. what you're saying is?"

"You will be brought back once more, through me. We will control your body together, as one being, rather than me simply being in your mind. Do you remember the battle in Tamiba City?"

"Ahh...! So, I'll be able to get the power I had then?"

"Heh... that was but a fraction of the full power I possess. This time, the

situation is much more dire. Compared to what you're about to become,

what happened in Tamiba City was nothing."

"You've got me pumped up Oritula!"

"Now, close your eyes, and when you wake up, you'll reach a state of

power no mortal has ever experienced before, not even Mai."

"Will do."

Naomi opened her eyes. No - Naomi and Oritula opened their eyes. Gee, this is confusing… Let's just call them Natula. Natula looked at herself, and realized she was now golden, and wearing a baby blue toga. Her eyes were entirely black. She got up and looked around, only to see that there wasn't a single soul left on the island. Everyone was dead. Natula began to break down, curling into a ball. She was all alone. But she was two, so she wasn't truly alone. She quickly pulled herself together, and began searching for Solituno. Solituno found them first, however.

Solituno came from behind, and swooped in behind Natula, dropping on the ground, **"How... I killed you! How are** you standing? Wrahgh, these forms are of no use to me! I'm going back into my TRUE form!"

Natula stared straight into the eyes of Solituno's lion head, as it steadily shrunk, and shrunk, until it became the head of a dark blue tabby cat with yellow eyes, dressed in a red toga.

"Solituno, embodiment of destruction, vengeance, evil, uhhh all that is bad. I will not be put to rest until you are defeated, for all eternity!"

"Oritula...? Heh, You've grown so weak, so pathetic, that you need to use a MORTAL as a vessel to make a last minute attempt to save this land you so love. Your fate will be a tragic one. I will never lose to you again."

Solituno lifted its palm into the sky. Then, a large force of darkness collected into a giant ball of toxic haze. Solituno then blew the haze towards Natula, and the smoke took her down to her knees, gasping for air. Solituno then jumped far into the sky, then flew straight into the ground, right on top of Natula.

"Such a sad way to go. If only you put up more of a fight, maybe then

you could 've beaten me! Just maybe! Haha!"

Solituno started rising up from the ground.

"Wha—what 's happening?!?"

Natula was holding Solituno (as heavy as it still was even with being brought to its true form), with one hand. Natula then threw Solituno up into the sky, jumped up along with them and slapped Solituno into the ground like a volleyball, leaving a large crater in the ground. Solituno begrudgingly jumped back up, and charged at full speed towards Natula, fist first. Natula blocked Solituno with her palm, and the impact was so loud that, if anyone else was left living in Mai, they would've heard the slap in any region.

Solituno tried its best to overpower Natula, pushing harder and harder, but Natula was unphased. Then, the eyes of Natula began to light up like a solar eclipse, and the light moved from her eyes to her palm. Solituno tried to get her palm off of their head, but it was almost like they were fused together.

"THIS... THIS MUST BE THE FUSION TOUCH."

And once more, everything turned blank.

HERMAN 191 HARRISON

THE VOID

"**W**hat is the meaning of this? Where am I? Get me out of

here!"

"Hello, Solituno."

"...Why have I been sent here?"

"We are now fused into one, so that you may never do any harm to

those in the physical realm again."

"Is that so? Haha... HA HA!"

"Hey, what's so funny huh?"

"In your efforts to null my influence on the physical realm, you bring

yourself to the very place I'm in! OF NO USE! If I can't roam the

physical world, neither can you!"

"Losing my ability to go into the physical realm again, to save the

people of Mai from the likes of you, is a pleasure."

"Hehe... fool... You're bringing yourself down to stop me. How

selfless."

"Solituno, isn't that what you have done? In an effort to destroy everything around you, you have lost who you are."

"What do you mean? I am meant to destroy you! I am meant to destroy everything WITH YOU! I am simply doing what I have been placed here to do!"

"Solituno, Solituno... You are not here to destroy me, but to keep the delicate balance of creation and destruction, so that the universe may stay in existence. I'm doing my part as well. You really think I'm not just as capable of seeking you out to take you out from existence?"

"Hah! As if you could do that. Tell me, what does this so—called 'delicate balance' of the universe mean to you? Me? Oritula, come on. Join me, and we can rule the universe together! Why do you care so much for these mortals?"

"I care for them because they are all there is worth existing for. Without life, there is no reason for our existence. Don't you see? Even you play a role in the cycle of life. You bring upon death, which leaves room for more life to be brought to the world, like how mushrooms feed off of dead trees. You brought the crocodilian race to the Land of Mai as well."

"But... If life is so important, and It's supposed to be our very reason

for existing — to bring about life... Why am I able to destroy?"

"Maybe you ARE here to destroy... But you don't HAVE to destroy. Not for

any good reason, at least. You don't have to strive to hurt others. You

can rest, Solituno. There is no more fighting to do. Your purpose is the

one you make, don't you see? ...Have I made you see your faults?"

"...Hah. Hundreds of thousands of millenia existing with the

preconceived notion, that I was here only to destroy all that I could.

An ever growing hatred for everything around me, and I never

thought for a moment, what exactly the purpose was of all of this."

"It is never too late to redefine your purpose, Solituno. Even... Even a

beaver can choose whether or not to destroy a tree!"

"Heh...well, I guess I don't mind doing that. I've hurt many people.

I've destroyed so much. What do I do now?"

"Well, I guess we'll figure that out when we come back to Mai."

"And when will that be?"

"Now."

HERMAN 194 HARRISON

Natula was now fused with Solituno. Let's give

them a new name… Ahh yes, I believe Natulo will do.

Beautiful, a perfect balance. He was splotched with gold and

purple fur, and had white eyes, making it look like he had no

pupils. When Natulo woke up, he arose to the devastating

sight of nothing but destruction all around him.

"I… I did all of this? I must fix this… somehow, someway."

Natulo possessed the power of healing, and sought to

fix his mistakes. He then spun up into the atmosphere, so far

into the sky he could see all of Mai. "I will fix this destruction

that I have caused…"

Natulo then swiveled around, spreading sprinkles of

life energy, then blew them down to Mai, reaching every

corner of Mai, as well as the island of Mai.

The sparkles swooped around in the wind, and when

they landed on the destroyed land, plants began to sprout,

creating new forests where they had been destroyed. And what

was most astonishing of all, was that when the sparkles

touched the body of a dead creature, they sprung back to life.

Not like lifeless puppets, no. Their souls were brought back to their bodies once more.

"I believe I have righted my wrongs."

Makim woke up on the ground, "Man... wait -

what happened? Why is everything back to normal?

Manny!"

Manny was beside Makim, "Hey! How... How are

we still alive? I thought we died."

Makim caught a sparkle speeding down to the ground

from what seemed like space. When it landed, Makim focused

on it and realized it was Naomi... Well, Natulo.

"Naomi! I knew you could defeat Solituno! We're

saved! Uh... what happened to you? Why're you purple

and gold?"

"Makim my friend, I am no longer just Naomi. I am Naomi, I

am Oritula, and I am Solituno. I am Natulo."

"What? How? So... Am I speaking to all of you at once?"

"Yes, we are now one."

Manny ran up to Natulo after talking to the locals,

"Hey, Naomi- I mean, Natulo! The townspeople want to thank you for saving the whole world. They're gonna have a festival in your honor!"

Natulo's chest began to bulge, "I'm sorry, but I cannot stay. It seems, that all of us hosting this one body, wasn't exactly the most stable way to be in the physical realm."

"Well, is there any way we can help you? Maybe we could-"

"Manny, there is nothing you or anyone can do. My body is dissipating. Where we will go after, I don't know. I have righted my wrongs, and I may now rest in peace."

Makim knocked himself into the conversation, "Naomi come on! I know you can find a way to stay here! Don't just let go like that! You've fought so hard to keep Mai safe, you deserve to be here to see it in peace!"

"Makim. I am not Naomi. I am Natulo."

Natulo's body started turning transparent, "I'm afraid I don't have much time, friends. I'm proud of you all. Though I'm not entirely sure that we'll ever see each other again, Do know, that I will always be with you, in spirit."

"Naomi..."

Natulo's body began phasing completely out. Makim tried grabbing onto him, but his hands went straight through his body.

Manny tried to comfort him, "Makim, don't be sad."

"Yeah, like I can do that right now. How could she just, just dip out on us like that? Just out of the blue, 'Oh I've got to go, bye guys, I guess I'll never see you ever again!'"

"It's not like she wanted to leave us Makim. *sigh*, You know Makim, this was always how it was gonna end for her. This was her destiny, her purpose in life. To save us all from the forces of destruction. Makim, I think you know very well Naomi wouldn't want you to be here sulking over her! She'd want you to be happy! Look around you man, there's nothing left to fight, no problems left to face. We can finally relax."

"I guess I understand. But that doesn't make me miss her any less."

"I know Makim. I know."

Makim and Manny left the island of Mai to return to

Tamiba City, to figure out what was next for them.

Now, I'm not sure where Naomi is now. I don't know

where Oritula or Solituno are. I mean, they can't die, so are

they in another universe? Reincarnated? Well, I have no clue

on that, but one thing I know for sure, is that wherever Naomi

is, I'm sure she's looking for a new adventure.

www.ingramcontent.com/pod-product-compliance
Lightning Source LLC
Chambersburg PA
CBHW021438150726
47989CB00001B/293